Excer

From “ ... Ants”

“Leining... he shouted. “You're insane! They're not creatures you can fight—they're an act of God! Ten miles long, two miles wide—ants, nothing but ants! And every single one of them a fiend from hell; before you can spit three times, they'll eat a full-grown buffalo to the bones. I tell you, if you don't clear out at once, there'll he nothing left of you but a skeleton picked as clean as your own plantation.”

From “The Most Dangerous Game”

“I wanted the ideal animal to hunt,” explained the general. “So I said, ‘What are the attributes of an ideal quarry?’ And the answer was, of course, ‘It must have courage, cunning, and, above all, it must be able to reason.’ ”

“But no animal can reason,” objected Rainsford.

“My dear fellow,” said the general, “there is one that can.”

Edited by
Beth Johnson and Barbara Solot

Afterword by Beth Johnson

THE TOWNSEND LIBRARY

GREAT STORIES OF SUSPENSE AND ADVENTURE

TP THE TOWNSEND LIBRARY

For more titles in the Townsend Library,
visit our website: **www.townsendpress.com**

Printed in the United States of America.

0 9 8 7 6

ISBN-13: 978-1-59194-000-5
ISBN-10: 1-59194-000-1

Library of Congress Control Number:
2002114605

TABLE OF CONTENTS

PREVIEW

Rikki-Tikki-Tavi is a mongoose by birth and a snake-killer by profession. He thinks he has found the perfect home when he is adopted by a human family. But that's before he learns about Nag and Nagaina, the dangerous cobras that live in the garden. The cobras, Nag and Nagaina soon have Rikki—and his human friends—marked for death.

RIKKI-TIKKI-TAVI

Rudyard Kipling

This is the story of the great war that Rikki-Tikki-Tavi fought single-handedly, through the bathrooms of a big bungalow. Darzee, the tailorbird, helped him. Chuchundra, the muskrat, who never comes out into the middle of the floor, but always creeps around by the wall, gave him advice. But Rikki-Tikki-Tavi did the real fighting.

Rikki-Tikki-Tavi was a mongoose—his fur and his tail rather like a cat's, but his head and his habits quite like a weasel's. His eyes and the end of his restless nose were pink. He could scratch himself anywhere he pleased, with any leg he chose to use, front or back. He could fluff up his tail till it looked like a brush. And as he scuttled through the long grass, his war cry was *Rikk-tikk-tikki-tikki-tichk*!

One summer day, a flood washed him out of the burrow where he lived with his mother and father and carried him kicking and clucking down a roadside ditch. He found a little wisp of grass floating there, and clung to it till he lost consciousness. When he revived, he was lying in the hot sun in the middle of a garden path, very wet, dirty, and tired indeed. A small boy was saying, "Here's a dead mongoose. Let's have a funeral."

"No," said his mother. "Let's take him in and dry him. Perhaps he isn't really dead."

They took him into the house and a big man picked him up between his finger and thumb and said he was not dead at all but half choked. They wrapped him in a blanket and warmed him over a small fire. He opened his eyes and sneezed.

"Now," said the big man, "don't frighten him, and we'll see what he'll do."

It is the hardest thing in the world to frighten a mongoose, because he is eaten up with curiosity from his nose to his tail. The motto of all the mongoose family is, "Run and find out," and Rikki-Tikki was a true mongoose. He looked at the blanket, decided that it was not good to eat, ran all around the table, sat up, smoothed his fur, scratched himself, and jumped on the small boy's shoulder.

"Don't be frightened, Teddy," said his father. "That's his way of making friends."

"Oooh! He's tickling under my chin," said Teddy.

Rikki-Tikki looked down between the boy's collar and neck, sniffed at his ear, and climbed down to the floor, where he sat rubbing his nose.

"Good gracious," said Teddy's mother, "that's a wild creature? I suppose he's so tame because we've been kind to him."

"All mongooses are like that," said her husband. "If Teddy doesn't pick him up by the tail, or try to put him in a cage, he'll run in and out of the house all day long. Let's give him something to eat."

They gave him a little piece of raw meat. Rikki-Tikki liked it immensely. When it was finished, he went out onto the veranda, sat in the sunshine, and fluffed up his fur to make it dry to the roots. Then he felt better.

"There are more things to find out about in this house than all my family could find out in all their lives," he said to himself. "I shall certainly stay and find out."

He spent all that day roaming around the house. He nearly drowned himself in the bathtubs. He put his nose into the ink on a writing table and burned it on the end of the big man's cigar when he climbed into his lap to watch how writing was done. At nightfall he ran into Teddy's nursery to watch how kerosene lamps were lighted. And when Teddy went to bed, Rikki-Tikki climbed up there too. But he was a restless companion because he had to check out every noise all through the night to find out what made it. Teddy's mother and father came in, the last thing in the evening, to look at their boy, and Rikki-Tikki was awake on the pillow.

"I don't like that," said Teddy's mother; "he may bite the child."

"He'll do no such thing," said the father. "Teddy's safer with that little beast than if he had a bloodhound to watch him. If a snake came into the nursery now . . ."

But Teddy's mother wouldn't think of anything so awful.

Early in the morning, Rikki-Tikki came to breakfast on the veranda, riding on Teddy's shoulder. They gave him a banana and some boiled eggs, and he sat on all their laps one after the other because a very-well-brought-up mongoose always hopes to someday be a house mongoose and have rooms to run about in. Rikki-Tikki's mother had carefully taught Rikki what to do if he ever got the chance to live in a house with people.

Then Rikki-Tikki went out into the garden to see what was to be seen. It was a large garden, with bushes as big as houses, lime and orange trees, clumps of bamboo, and thickets of high grass. Rikki-Tikki licked his lips.

"This is a splendid hunting ground," he said, and his tail grew thick and bushy at the thought of it. He scuttled up and down the garden, sniffing here and there till he heard very sorrowful voices in a thornbush. It was Darzee, the tailorbird, and his wife. They had made a beautiful nest by pulling two big leaves together, stitching them up the edges with fibers, and filling the hollow with cotton and downy fluff. The nest swayed to and fro as they sat on the rim and cried.

"What's the matter?" asked Rikki-Tikki.

"We are very miserable," said Darzee. "One of our babies fell out of the nest yesterday and Nag ate him."

"Hmmmm!" said Rikki-Tikki, "that is

very sad—but I am a stranger here. Who is Nag?"

Darzee and his wife cowered down in the nest without answering, for from the thick grass at the foot of the bush there came a low hiss—a horrid sound that made Rikki-Tikki jump back two feet. Then inch by inch out of the grass rose up the head and spread hood of Nag, the big black cobra. He was five feet long from tongue to tail. When he had lifted one-third of himself up—clear of the ground—he stayed swaying to and fro, exactly like a dandelion sways in the wind. He looked at Rikki-Tikki with the wicked eyes of a snake that never change their expression, whatever the snake may be thinking.

"What is Nag?" he said. "I am Nag. The great God Brahma put his mark upon all cobras when the first cobra spread his hood to keep the sun off Brahma as he slept. Look and be afraid!"

He spread out his hood more than ever, and Rikki-Tikki saw a grand marking on the back of it. It looked exactly like the eye part of a hook-and-eye fastening. He was afraid for a minute, but it is impossible for a mongoose to stay frightened for any length of time. And though Rikki-Tikki had never met a live cobra before, his mother had fed him on dead ones. He knew that a grown mongoose's business in life was to fight and eat snakes. Nag knew that too, and at the bottom of his cold heart, he was afraid.

"Well," he said, as his tail began to fluff up again, "marks or no marks, do you think it's right for you to eat baby birds out of a nest?"

Nag was thinking to himself and watching the least little movement in the grass behind Rikki-Tikki. He knew that mongooses in the garden meant death, sooner or later, for him and his family. He wanted to get Rikki-Tikki off his guard, so he dropped his head a little, leaning it to one side.

"Let us talk," he said. "You eat eggs. Why should I not eat birds?"

"Behind you! Look behind you!" sang Darzee.

Rikki-Tikki knew better than to waste time staring. He jumped up in the air as high as he could go, and just under him whizzed by the head of Nagaina, Nag's wicked wife. She had crept up behind him to kill him. He heard her savage hiss as her stroke missed and he came down almost across her back. If he had been an older mongoose, he would have known that then was the time to break her back with one bite, but he was afraid of the terrible lashing return-stroke of the cobra. He bit, indeed, but did not bite long enough. And he jumped clear of her whisking tail, leaving Nagaina torn and angry.

"Wicked, wicked Darzee!" said Nag, reaching up as high as he could toward the nest in the thornbush; but Darzee had built it out of reach of snakes, and it only swayed to and fro.

Rikki-Tikki felt his eyes growing red and hot (when a mongoose's eyes grow red, he is angry). He sat back on his tail and hind legs like a small kangaroo and looked all around him, chattering with rage. But Nag and Nagaina had disappeared into the grass. When a snake misses its stroke, it never says anything or gives any sign of what it means to do next. Rikki-Tikki did not care to follow them, for he did not feel sure that he could manage two snakes at one time. So he trotted off to the gravel path near the house and sat down to think. This was a serious matter for him. If you read the old books of natural history, you will find they say that when the mongoose fights the snake and happens to get bitten, he runs off and eats some herb that cures him. That is not true. The victory is only a matter of quickness of eye and quickness of foot—a snake's strike against the mongoose's jump. And as no eye can follow the motion of a snake's head when it strikes, this makes things much more wonderful than any magic herb. Rikki-Tikki knew he was a young mongoose, and it made him all the more pleased to think that he had managed to escape a blow from behind. It gave him confidence in himself, and when Teddy came running down the path, Rikki-Tikki was ready to be petted. But just as Teddy was stooping down, something wriggled a little in the dust, and a tiny voice said: "Be careful. I am Death!" It was Karait, the dusty brown snakeling that lies in the dusty earth. His bite is as dangerous as the cobra's, but he is so small that nobody gives him a thought, and so he does much more harm to people.

Rikki-Tikki's eyes grew red again, and he danced up to Karait with the peculiar rocking, swaying motion he had inherited from his family. It looks very funny, but it is so perfectly balanced a gait that he can fly off and attack from any angle he pleases. In dealing with snakes, this is an advantage. If Rikki-Tikki had only known . . . he was doing a much more dangerous thing than fighting Nag, for Karait is so small, and can turn so quickly, that unless Rikki bit him close to the back of the head, the snake would strike in return, hitting his eye or lip.

But Rikki did not know this: his eyes were all red and he rocked back and forth, looking for a good place to grab hold. Karait struck out. Rikki jumped sideways and tried to dodge the strike, but the wicked little dusty gray head lashed within a fraction of his shoulder. Rikki had to jump over the body, and the snake's head followed closely on his heels.

Teddy shouted into the house. "Oh look here, our mongoose is killing a snake!" And Rikki-Tikki heard a scream from Teddy's mother. His father ran out with a stick, but by the time he got there, Karait had lunged out once too far. Rikki-Tikki-Tavi had sprung, jumped on the snake's back, dropped his head far between his forelegs, bitten as high up on the snake's back as he could get hold, and then rolled away. This bite paralyzed Karait, and Rikki-Tikki was going to eat him up from the tail as was the custom of his family at dinner. Then he remembered that a full meal makes a slow mongoose. If he wanted all his strength and quickness, he must keep himself thin. He went away to bathe in the dust under the bushes, while Teddy's father beat the dead Karait.

"What's the use of that?" thought Rikki-Tikki. "I have finished it all." And then

Teddy's mother picked him up from the dust and hugged him, crying that he had saved Teddy from death. Teddy's father said he was a blessing. And Teddy looked on with big, scared eyes. Rikki-Tikki was rather amused at all the fuss, which, of course, he did not understand. Teddy's mother might just as well have petted Teddy for playing in the dust. Rikki was thoroughly enjoying himself.

That night at dinner, walking up and back among the wineglasses on the table, he might have stuffed himself three times over with nice things. But he remembered Nag and Nagaina and though it was very pleasant to be petted by Teddy's mother, and to sit on Teddy's shoulder. From time to time his eyes would get red, and he would sound off with his long war cry of *Rikk-tikk-tikki-tikki-tchk*!

Teddy carried him off to bed and insisted that Rikki-Tikki sleep under his chin. Rikki-Tikki was too well-bred to bite or scratch, but as soon as Teddy was asleep, he went off for his nightly walk around the house. In the dark, he ran into Chuchundra, the muskrat, creeping around by the wall. Chuchundra is a broken-hearted little beast. He whimpers and chirps all night long, trying to make up his mind to run into the middle of the room, but he never gets there.

"Don't kill me," said Chuchundra, almost weeping. "Rikki-Tikki, don't kill me!"

"Do you think a snake-killer kills muskrats?" Rikki-Tikki said scornfully.

"Those who kill snakes get killed by snakes," said Chuchundra, more sorrowfully than ever. "And how can I be sure that Nag won't mistake me for you some dark night?"

"There's not the least danger," said Rikki-Tikki. "Nag is in the garden, and I know you don't go there."

"My cousin, Chua, the rat told me—" said Chuchundra, and then he stopped.

"Told you what?"

"Hush! Nag is everywhere, Rikki-Tikki. You should have talked to Chua in the garden."

"I didn't, so you must tell me. Quick, Chuchundra, or I'll bite you."

Chuchundra sat down and cried till the tears rolled off his whiskers. "I am a very poor muskrat," he sobbed. "I never had enough spirit to run out into the middle of the room. Hush! I mustn't tell you anything. Can't you hear, Rikki-Tikki?"

Rikki-Tikki listened. The house was as still as still, but he thought he could just catch the faintest scratch-scratch in the world. A noise as faint as that of a wasp walking on a windowpane—the dry scratch of a snake's scales on brickwork.

"That's Nag or Nagaina," he said to himself, "and he is crawling into the bathroom drain. You're right, Chuchundra. I should have talked to Chua."

He stole off to Teddy's bathroom, but there was nothing there. And then to Teddy's mother's bathroom. At the bottom of the smooth plaster wall, there was a brick pulled out to make a drain for the bathwater, and as Rikki-Tikki snuck in by the bathtub, he heard Nag and Nagaina whispering together outside in the moonlight.

"When the house is emptied of people," said Nagaina to her husband, "he will have to go away, and then the garden will be our own again. Go in quietly, and remember that the big man who killed Karait is the first one to bite. Then come out and tell me, and we will hunt Rikki-Tikki together."

"But are you sure that there is anything to be gained by killing the people?" said Nag.

"Everything. When there were no people in the house, did we have any mongoose in the garden? As long as the house is empty, we are king and queen of the garden. And remember, as soon as our eggs in the melon bed hatch (as they may tomorrow), our children will need room and quiet."

"I had not thought of that," said Nag. "I will go, but there is no need to hunt for Rikki-Tikki afterward. I will kill the big man and his wife and the child if I can, and come away quietly. Then the house will be empty, and Rikki-Tikki will go away."

Rikki-Tikki tingled all over with rage and hatred at this. And then Nag's head came through the drain, and his five feet of cold body followed it. Angry as he was, Rikki-Tikki was very frightened as he saw the size of the big cobra. Nag coiled himself up, raised his head, and looked into the bathroom in the dark. Rikki could see his eyes glitter.

"Now if I kill him here, Nagaina will know; and if I fight him on the open floor, the odds are in his favor. What am I to do?" said Rikki-Tikki.

Nag waved to and fro, and then Rikki-Tikki heard him drinking from the water jar that was used to fill the bath. "That is good," said the snake. "Now when Karait was killed, the big man had a stick. He may still have that stick. But when he comes to bathe in the morning, he surely will not have a stick. I shall wait here until he comes. Nagaina—do you hear me?—I shall wait here where it's cool till daytime."

There was no answer from outside, so

Rikki-Tikki knew Nagaina had gone away. Nag coiled himself down, coil by coil, and wrapped himself around the bottom of the water jar. Rikki-Tikki stayed as still as death. After an hour he began to move, muscle by muscle, toward the jar. Nag was asleep, and Rikki-Tikki looked at his big back, wondering which would be the best place to attack and grab hold. "If I don't break his back at the first jump," said Rikki, "he can still fight; and if he fights, oh Rikki!" He looked at the thickness of the snake's neck, below the hood, but that was too much for him. And a bite near the tail would only make Nag savage.

"I must go for the head," he said at last, "the head above the hood; and once I am there, I must not let go,"

Then he jumped at the snake. Nag's head was lying just clear of the water jar, and as his teeth met, Rikki braced his back against the jar to hold down the head. This gave him one extra second, and he made the most of it. Then he was battered to and fro, as the snake fought his grip. Back and forth on the floor, up and down and around in great circles. But his eyes were red and he held on as his body was whipped over the floor and banged against the side of the bathtub. He held on and closed his jaws tighter and tighter. He was sure he would be banged to death, and for the honor of his family, he preferred to be found with his teeth locked. He was dizzy and aching and felt shaken to pieces when something went off like a thunderclap just behind him. A hot wind knocked him senseless, and red fire singed his fur. The big man had been wakened by the noise and had fired both barrels of his shotgun into Nag just behind the hood.

Rikki-Tikki held on tight with his eyes shut, for now he was quite sure he was dead. The snake's head did not move, and the big man picked him up and said, "It's the mongoose again, Alice. The little chap has saved our lives now." Teddy's mother came in with a very white face and saw what was left of Nag. Rikki-Tikki dragged himself to Teddy's bedroom and spent half the night shaking himself tenderly to find out whether he really was broken into forty pieces as he imagined.

When morning came he was very stiff, but well pleased with what he had done. "Now I have Nagaina to settle with, and she will be worse than five Nags. And there's no way of knowing when the eggs she spoke of will hatch. Goodness! I must go and see Darzee," he said.

Without waiting for breakfast, Rikki-Tikki ran to the thornbush where Darzee was singing a song of triumph at the top of his voice. The news of Nag's death was already all over the garden because the body had been thrown in the rubbish heap.

"Oh, you stupid tuft of feathers!" said Rikki-Tikki angrily. "Is this the time to sing?"

"Nag is dead—is dead—is dead!" sang Darzee. "The valiant Rikki-Tikki caught him by the head and held fast. The big man brought the bangstick and Nag fell in two pieces! He will never eat my babies again."

"All that's true enough, but where's Nagaina?" said Rikki-Tikki, looking carefully around him.

"Nagaina came to the bathroom drain and called for Nag," Darzee went on, "and Nag came out on the end of a stick—thrown on the rubbish heap. Let us sing about the great red-eyed Rikki-Tikki-Tavi!" and Darzee filled his throat and sang.

"If I could get up to your nest, I'd throw your babies out!" said Rikki-Tikki. "You don't know when to do the right thing at the right time. You're safe enough in your nest there, but it's war for me down here. Stop singing for a minute, Darzee."

"For the great, beautiful Rikki-Tikki-

Tavi's sake, I will stop," said Darzee. "What is it, oh killer of the terrible Nag?"

"Again I ask, where is Nagaina?"

"On the rubbish heap by the stables, mourning for Nag. Great is Rikki-Tikki with the white teeth!"

"Forget my white teeth! Have you heard where she keeps her eggs?"

"In the melon bed, on the end nearest the wall, where the sun shines nearly all day. She hid them there weeks ago."

"And you never thought it worthwhile to tell me? The end nearest the wall, you said?"

"Rikki-Tikki, you are not going to eat her eggs?"

"Not eat exactly, Darzee, no. If you have a grain of sense, you will fly off to the stables and pretend that your wing is broken and let Nagaina chase you away to this bush. I must go to the melon bed, and if I went there now, she'd see me."

Darzee was a feather-brained little fellow who could never keep more than one idea in his head at a time. Just because he knew that Nagaina's children were born in eggs like his own, he didn't think, at first, that it was fair to kill them. But his wife was a sensible bird, and she knew that cobra's eggs meant young cobras later on. So she flew off from the nest and left Darzee to keep the babies warm and continue his song about the death of Nag.

She fluttered in front of Nagaina by the rubbish heap and cried out, "Oh, my wing is broken! The boy in the house threw a stone at me and broke it." Then she fluttered more desperately than ever.

Nagaina lifted up her head and hissed, "You warned Rikki-Tikki when I would have killed him. Indeed and truly, you've chosen a bad place to come with a broken wing." And she moved toward Darzee's wife, sliding along the dust.

"The boy broke it with a stone!" shrieked Darzee's wife.

"Well! It may be some consolation to you, to know that when you're dead I shall settle accounts with the boy. My husband lies on the rubbish heap this morning, and before nightfall, the boy too will be still. What is the use of running away? I am sure to catch you. Little fool, look at me!"

Darzee's wife knew better than to do that, for a bird who looks in a snake's eyes gets so frightened that she cannot move. Darzee's wife fluttered on, piping sorrowfully and never leaving the ground, and Nagaina quickened her pace.

Rikki-Tikki heard them going up the

path from the stables, and he raced to the end of the melon bed near the wall. There, very cunningly hidden, he found twenty-five eggs, about the size of a small bird's eggs, but with whitish skins instead of shells.

"I was not a day too soon," he said, for he could see the baby cobras curled up inside the skin, and he knew that the minute they were hatched, they could each kill a man or a mongoose. He bit off the tops of the eggs as fast as he could, taking care to crush the young cobras, and turned over the litter from time to time to see whether he had missed any. At last there were only three eggs left, and Rikki-Tikki began to chuckle to himself, when he heard Darzee's wife screaming:

"Rikki-Tikki, I led Nagaina toward the house, and she has gone onto the veranda, and—oh, come quickly—she means killing!"

Rikki-Tikki smashed two eggs, tumbled backward down the melon bed with the third egg in his mouth, and scuttled to the veranda as fast as he could put foot to the ground. Teddy and his mother and father were there at early breakfast, but Rikki-Tikki saw that they were not eating anything. They sat stone-still, and their faces were white. Nagaina was coiled up on the matting by Teddy's chair, within easy striking distance of

Teddy's bare leg, and she was swaying to and fro, singing a song of triumph.

"Son of the big man that killed Nag," she hissed, "stay still. I am not ready yet. Wait a little. Keep very still, all you three! If you move, I strike; and if you do not move, I strike. Oh, foolish people who killed my Nag!"

Teddy's eyes were fixed on his father, and all his father could do was to whisper, "Sit still, Teddy. You mustn't move. Teddy, keep still."

Then Rikki-Tikki came up and cried: "Turn around, Nagaina; turn and fight!"

"All in good time," she said without moving her eyes. "I will settle my account with you presently. Look at your friends, Rikki-Tikki. They are still and white. They are afraid. They dare not move, and if you come a step nearer, I strike."

"Look at your eggs," said Rikki-Tikki, "in the melon bed near the wall. Go and look, Nagaina!"

The big snake turned half around and saw the egg on the veranda. "Ah-h! Give it to me," she said.

Rikki-Tikki put his paws one on each side of the egg, and his eyes were blood-red. "What price for a snake's egg? For a young cobra? For a young king-cobra? For the last—the very last of the brood? The ants are eating all the others down by the melon bed."

Nagaina spun clear around, forgetting everything for the sake of the one egg, and Rikki-Tikki saw Teddy's father shoot out a big hand, grab Teddy by the shoulder, and drag him across the table, safe and out of reach of Nagaina.

"Tricked! Tricked! Tricked! Rikk-tck-tck!" chuckled Rikki-Tikki. "The boy is safe, and it was I—I—I—that caught Nag by the hood last night in the bathroom." Then he began to jump up and down, all four feet together, his head close to the floor. "He threw me to and fro, but he could not shake me off. He was dead before the big man blew him in two. I did it! Rikki-tikki-tck-tck! Come then, Nagaina. Come and fight with me. You shall not be a widow long."

Nagaina saw that she had lost her chance of killing Teddy, and the egg lay between Rikki-Tikki's paws. "Give me the egg, Rikki-Tikki. Give me the last of my eggs and I will go away and never come back," she said, lowering her hood.

"Yes, you will go away, and you will never come back; for you will go to the rubbish heap with Nag. Fight, widow! The big man has gone for his gun! Fight!"

Rikki-Tikki was bounding all around Nagaina, keeping just out of reach of her stroke, his little eyes like hot coals. Nagaina gathered herself together and lunged out at him. Rikki-Tikki jumped up and backwards. Again and again and again she struck, and each time her head came down with a whack on the matting of the veranda and she gathered herself together like a watchspring. Then Rikki-Tikki danced in a little circle to get behind her, and Nagaina spun around to keep her head to his head, so that the rustle of her tail on the matting sounded like dry leaves blown along by the wind.

He had forgotten the egg. It still lay on the veranda, and Nagaina came nearer and nearer to it, till at last, while Rikki-Tikki was drawing breath, she caught it in her mouth, turned to the veranda steps, and flew like an arrow down the path with Rikki-Tikki behind her. When the cobra runs for her life, she goes like a whiplash flicked across a horse's neck. Rikki-Tikki knew that he must catch her, or all the trouble would begin again. She headed straight for the long grass by the thornbush, and as he was running, Rikki-Tikki heard Darzee still singing his foolish little song of triumph. But Darzee's wife was wiser. She flew off her nest as Nagaina came along, and flapped her wings about Nagaina's head. If Darzee had helped, they might have distracted her, but Nagaina only lowered her hood and went on. Still, the instant's delay brought Rikki-Tikki up to her, and as she plunged into the rat hole where she and Nag used to live, his little white teeth were clenched on her tail, and he went down with her. Very few mongooses, however wise and old they may be, care to follow a cobra into its hole. It was dark in the hole, and Rikki-Tikki never knew when it might open out and give Nagaina room to turn and strike at him. He held on savagely, and stuck out his feet to act as brakes on the dark slope of the hot, moist earth. Then the grass by the mouth of the hole stopped waving, and Darzee said: "It is all over for Rikki-Tikki!" We must sing his death song. Valiant Rikki-Tikki-Tavi is dead! For Nagaina will surely kill him underground."

So he sang a very mournful song that he made up on the spur of the moment, and just as he got to the most touching part, the grass quivered again, and Rikki-Tikki, covered with dirt, dragged himself out of the hole, leg by leg, licking his whiskers. Darzee stopped short with a little shout. Rikki-Tikki shook some of the dust out of his fur and sneezed.

"It's all over," he said. "The widow will never come out again." And the red ants that live between the grass stems heard him and began to troop down, one after another, to see if he had spoken the truth.

Rikki-Tikki curled himself up in the grass and slept where he was—slept and slept till it was late in the afternoon, for he had done a hard day's work.

"Now," he said, when he awoke, "I will go back to the house. Tell the Coppersmith, Darzee, and he will tell the garden that Nagaina is dead."

The Coppersmith is a bird who makes a noise exactly like the beating of a hammer on a copper pot. The reason he is always making it is that he is the town crier to every garden and tells the news to everybody who cares to listen. As Rikki-Tikki went up the path, he heard the Coppersmith's sound—like a tiny dinner gong—and then a steady "Ding-dong-tock! Nag is dead—dong! Nagaina is dead! Ding-dong-tock." That set all the birds in the garden singing, and the frogs croaking—for Nag and Nagaina used to eat frogs as well as little birds.

When Rikki got to the house, Teddy and Teddy's mother and father came out and almost cried with joy over him. And that night he ate all that was given to him, till he could eat no more, and went to bed on Teddy's shoulder where Teddy's mother saw him when she came in late that night.

"He saved our lives and Teddy's life," she said to her husband. "Just think, he saved all our lives!"

Rikki-Tikki woke up with a jump, for mongooses are light sleepers.

"Oh, it's you," he said. "What are you worrying about? All the cobras are dead; and if they weren't, I'm here."

Rikki-Tikki had a right to be proud of himself. But he did not grow too proud, and he kept that garden as a mongoose should keep it—with tooth and jump and spring and bite, so a cobra never dared to show its head inside the walls. ■

PREVIEW

If you were magically granted three wishes, how wonderful it would be ... wouldn't it? Or is there a price to be paid for wishes come true? A kindly old couple has the chance to find out in this classic tale of horror and suspense.

THE MONKEY'S PAW

W.W. Jacobs

Outside, the night was cold and wet, but in the small living room the blinds were drawn and the fire burned brightly. Father and son were playing chess. The old man, who was a reckless player, often put his king into such unnecessary danger that even his white-haired wife, knitting peacefully by the fire, commented on it.

"Listen to that wind," said Mr. White. Having seen a fatal mistake after it was too late, he tried to keep his son from noticing it.

"I'm listening," said the son, studying the board as he stretched out his hand. "Check."

"I doubt that he'll come tonight," said his father, with his hand poised over the board.

"Checkmate," replied the son.

"That's the worst thing about living so far out of town," exclaimed Mr. White, with sudden and unexpected bad temper. "Of all the beastly, slushy, out-of-the-way places to live in, this is the worst. The pathway is a bog, and the road's a river. I don't know what people are thinking about. I suppose because only two houses on the road have anyone in them, they think it doesn't matter."

"Never mind, dear," said his wife soothingly; "perhaps you'll win the next one."

Mr. White looked up sharply, just in time to catch an amused glance between mother and son. The words died away on his lips, and he hid a guilty grin in his thin gray beard.

"There he is," said Herbert White, as the gate banged loudly and heavy footsteps came toward the door.

The old man rose quickly to meet the visitor. As he opened the door, he was heard sympathizing about the weather with the new arrival. He re-entered the room, followed by a tall, burly man with a red face and beady eyes.

Mr. White introduced the visitor. "Sergeant Major Morris," he said.

The sergeant major shook hands. Taking the seat he was offered by the fire, he watched happily while his host got out whiskey and glasses and put a small copper kettle on the fire.

At the third glass of whiskey, his eyes got brighter and he began to talk. The little family listened with eager interest to this visitor from foreign lands. He told them about strange scenes and daring deeds, of wars and disasters and strange peoples.

"Twenty-one years of it," said Mr. White, nodding at his wife and son. "When he went away, he was a skinny boy in the warehouse. Now look at him."

"He don't look like it's done him any harm," said Mrs. White politely.

"I'd like to go to India myself," said the old man, "just to look round a bit, you know."

"Better where you are," said the sergeant major, shaking his head. He put down the empty glass, and sighing softly, shook it again.

"I should like to see those old temples and holy men and jugglers," said the old man. "What was that you started telling me the other day about a monkey's paw or something, Morris?"

"Nothing," said the soldier hastily. "Anyway, nothing worth hearing."

"Monkey's paw?" said Mrs. White curiously.

"Well, it's just a bit of what you might call magic, perhaps," said the sergeant major offhandedly.

His three listeners leaned forward eagerly. The visitor absentmindedly put his empty glass to his lips and then set it down again. His host filled it for him.

"To look at," said the sergeant major, fumbling in his pocket, "it's just an ordinary little paw, dried like a mummy's."

He took something out of his pocket and offered it. Mrs. White drew back, making a face, but her son took it and examined it curiously.

"And what is there special about it?" asked Mr. White, as he took it from his son. After he looked at it, he placed it upon the table.

"It had a spell put on it by an old priest," said the sergeant major, "a very holy man. He wanted to show that fate ruled people's lives, and that those who interfered with it would be sorry they had. He put a spell on it so that three different men could each have three wishes from it."

His manner was so impressive that his listeners realized their laughter seemed out of place.

"Well, why don't you have three wishes, sir?" said Herbert White lightly.

The soldier regarded him in the way that middle-aged people often look at foolish youths. "I have," he said quietly, and his red face grew pale.

"And did you really have the three wishes granted?" asked Mrs. White.

"I did," said the sergeant major, and his glass tapped against his strong teeth.

"And has anybody else wished?" inquired the old lady.

"The first man had his three wishes, yes," was the reply. "I don't know what the first two were, but the third was for death. That's how I got the paw."

His tones were so serious that a hush fell upon the group.

"If you've had your three wishes, it's no good to you now, Morris," said the old man at last. "What do you keep it for?"

The soldier shook his head. "It's silly, I suppose," he said slowly. "I did have some idea of selling it, but I don't think I will. It has caused enough trouble already. Besides, people won't buy. They think it's a fairy tale, some of them, and those who do think anything of it want to try it first and pay me afterward."

"If you could have another three wishes," said the old man, looking at him hard, "would you have them?"

"I don't know," said the other. "I don't know."

He took the paw, and dangling it between his front finger and thumb, suddenly threw it upon the fire. White, with a slight cry, bent down and snatched it off.

"Better let it burn," said the soldier solemnly.

"If you don't want it, Morris," said the old man, "give it to me."

"I won't," said his friend stubbornly. "I threw it on the fire. If you keep it, don't blame me for what happens. Throw it on the fire again, like a sensible man."

The other shook his head and examined his new possession closely. "How do you do it?" he inquired.

"Hold it up in your right hand and wish aloud," said the sergeant major, "but I warn you against it."

"Sounds like the Arabian Nights," said

Mrs. White, as she rose and began to set the supper. "Don't you think you might wish for four pairs of hands for me?"

Her husband drew the paw from his pocket and then all three burst into laughter. The sergeant major, with a look of alarm on his face, caught him by the arm.

"If you must wish," he said gruffly, "wish for something sensible."

Mr. White dropped it back into his pocket and invited his friend to the table. In the business of supper the paw was partly forgotten, and afterward the three sat listening with great interest to more of the soldier's adventures in India.

"If he invented as much of the tale about the monkey's paw as he did those other stories, it won't do us much good," said Herbert, as the door closed behind their guest, just in time for him to catch the last train.

"Did you pay him anything for it, Father?" inquired Mrs. White.

"A little," he said, blushing slightly. "He didn't want it, but I made him take it. And he told me again to throw it away."

"Not likely!" said Herbert, with pretended horror. "Why, we're going to be rich, and famous, and happy. Wish to be an emperor,

Father, to begin with; then you can't be nagged."

He darted around the table, pursued by the insulted Mrs. White, armed with a dish-towel.

Mr. White took the paw from his pocket and eyed it doubtfully. "I don't know what to wish for, and that's a fact," he said slowly. "It seems to me I've got all I want."

"If you could pay off the house, you'd be quite happy, wouldn't you?" said Herbert, with his hand on his shoulder. "Well, wish for two thousand dollars, then; that'll just do it."

His father, smiling in some embarrassment at what he was doing, held up the paw. His son, with a solemn face but a comical wink at his mother, sat down at the piano and struck a few impressive chords.

"I wish for two thousand dollars," said the old man clearly.

A fine crash from the piano greeted the words, interrupted by a shuddering cry from the old man. His wife and son ran toward him.

"It moved," he cried, with a glance of disgust at the object as it lay on the floor. "As I wished, it twisted in my hand like a snake."

"Well, I don't see the money," said his son, as he picked it up and placed it on the table, "and I bet I never shall."

"It must have been your imagination, Father," said his wife, watching him anxiously.

He shook his head. "Never mind, though; there's no harm done, but it gave me a shock all the same."

They sat down by the fire again while the two men finished their pipes. Outside, the wind was higher than ever, and the old man jumped nervously at the sound of a door banging upstairs. A silence, unusual and depressing, settled upon all three. It lasted until the old couple started up to their room for the night.

"You'll probably find the cash tied up in a big bag in the middle of your bed," said Herbert, as he told them good night. "And something horrible will be sitting up on top of the dresser, watching you as you pocket your ill-gotten money."

Next morning, the wintry sun streamed brightly over the breakfast table. Herbert laughed at his fears. There was an air of ordinary goodness about the room which hadn't been there the night before. The dirty, wrinkled little paw was thrown on the side table in a careless way that showed no great belief in its power.

"I suppose all old soldiers are the same," said Mrs. White. "The idea of our listening to such nonsense! How could wishes be granted in these days? And if they could, how could two thousand dollars hurt you, Father?"

"It might drop on his head from the sky," said Herbert, chuckling.

"Morris said the things happened so naturally," said his father, "that you might think it was just a coincidence."

"Well, don't use up all the money before I come back," said Herbert, as he rose from the table. "I'm afraid it'll turn you into a mean, greedy man, and we shall have to send you away."

His mother laughed, and following him to the door, watched him down the road. Returning to the breakfast table, she made some gentle fun of her husband's wish of the night before. This did not prevent her from hurrying to the door when the mailman knocked. And when all that arrived was bills, she referred with some irritation to retired sergeant majors who drink too much.

"Herbert will have some more of his funny remarks, I expect, when he comes home," she said, as they sat at dinner.

"No doubt," said Mr. White, pouring himself out some beer; "but just the same, the thing moved in my hand; that I'll swear to."

"You thought it did," said the old lady soothingly.

"I say it did," replied the other. "There was no thought about it; I had just—What's the matter?"

His wife made no reply. She was watching the mysterious movements of a man outside. Staring at the house in an undecided fashion, he appeared to be trying to make up his mind whether to enter. With the two thousand dollars still on her mind, she noticed that the stranger was well dressed and wore a brand-new silk hat. Three times he paused at the gate, and then walked away again. The fourth time he stood with his hand upon it, and then flung it open and walked up the path. Mrs. White hurriedly untied the strings of her apron and hid it beneath the cushion of her chair.

She brought the stranger, a nervous-looking man, into the room. He didn't seem able to look directly at Mrs. White. As the old lady apologized for the untidiness of the room, and her husband's old coat, which he usually wore just for gardening, the man just stood there. She then waited as patiently as she could for him to explain his business, but he was at first strangely silent.

"I—was asked to come see you," he said at last, and stooped and picked a piece of cotton from his trousers. "I'm from the Maw and Meggins Company."

The old lady looked startled. "Is anything the matter?" she asked breathlessly. "Has anything happened to Herbert? What is it? What is it?"

Her husband interrupted. "There, there, Mother," he said hastily. "Sit down, and don't jump to conclusions. You haven't brought bad news, I'm sure, sir," and he eyed the other hopefully.

"I'm sorry—" began the visitor.

"Is he hurt?" demanded the mother.

The visitor nodded. "Badly hurt," he said quietly, "but he is no longer in any pain."

"Oh, thank God!" said the old woman, clasping her hands. "Thank God for that! Thank—"

She broke off suddenly as the dreadful meaning of his words dawned upon her. When he turned his face away, she saw that she was right. She caught her breath, and turning to her slower-witted husband, laid her trembling old hand upon his. There was a long silence.

"He was caught in the machinery," said the visitor finally, in a low voice.

"Caught in the machinery," repeated Mr. White, as if he were dreaming. "Yes."

He sat staring blankly out at the window. Taking his wife's hand between his own, he squeezed it as he used to do in their old courting days nearly forty years before.

"He was the only one left to us," he said, turning gently to the visitor. "It is hard."

The other coughed, and rising, walked slowly to the window. "The company wished me to express their sincere sympathy with you in your great loss," he said, without looking around. "Please understand I am only their servant and merely obeying orders."

There was no reply. The old woman's face was white, her eyes blank. She hardly seemed to be breathing. Her husband's face looked as a soldier's might as he entered his first battle.

"I was to say that Maw and Meggins have no responsibility for what happened," continued the other. "They are not to blame at all. But as your son was their employee, they wish to present you with a sum of money to assist you."

Mr. White dropped his wife's hand, and rising to his feet, gazed with a look of horror at his visitor. His dry lips shaped the words,

"How much?"

"Two thousand dollars," was the answer.

Not hearing his wife's shriek, the old man smiled faintly. He put out his hands like a blind man, and dropped, unconscious, to the floor.

In the huge new cemetery, two miles away, the old people buried their dead son. They came back to a house filled with shadow and silence. It was all over so quickly that at first they could hardly believe it. They kept expecting something else would happen, something that could lighten this load, too heavy for old hearts to bear. But the days passed, and they began to feel a hopeless acceptance. Sometimes they hardly exchanged a word, for now they had nothing to talk about. Their days were long and weary.

It was about a week later that the old man woke suddenly in the night and found himself alone. The room was in darkness, and the sound of quiet weeping came from the window. He raised himself in bed and listened.

"Come back," he said tenderly. "You will be cold."

"It is colder for my son," said the old

woman, and wept more.

The sound of her sobs died away on his ears. The bed was warm and his eyes heavy with sleep. He dozed on and off, and then slept until a sudden cry from his wife startled him.

"The monkey's paw!" she cried wildly. "The monkey's paw!"

He jumped up in alarm. "Where? Where is it? What's the matter?"

She came stumbling across the room toward him. "I want it," she said quietly. "You haven't destroyed it?"

"It's in the living room, on the table," he replied, confused. "Why?"

She cried and laughed at the same time, and bending over, kissed his cheek.

"I only just thought of it," she said excitedly. "Why didn't I think of it before? Why didn't you think of it?"

"Think of what?" he questioned.

"The other two wishes," she replied. "We've only had one."

"Wasn't that enough?" he demanded fiercely.

"No," she cried happily; "we'll have one more. Go down and get it quickly, and wish our boy alive again."

The man sat up in bed and flung the

blankets back. "Good God, you are mad!" he cried, horrified.

"Get it," she panted; "get it quickly, and wish—oh, my boy, my boy!"

Her husband struck a match and lit the candle. "Get back to bed," he said unsteadily. "You don't know what you are saying."

"We had the first wish granted," insisted the old woman; "why not the second?"

"It was a coincidence," stammered the old man.

"Go and get it and wish," cried the old woman, and dragged him toward the door.

He went down in the darkness and felt his way to the living room, and then to the little table. The paw was in its place. He was suddenly filled with horrible fear. Could his unspoken wish bring his son, horribly damaged, into the room before he could escape? In the dark he could not find the door, and his forehead grew cold with sweat. He felt his way around the table and along the wall until he found himself with the awful thing in his hand.

Even his wife's face seemed changed as he entered the room. It was white and expectant, and in his fears seemed to have an unnatural look upon it. He was afraid of her.

"Wish!" she cried, in a strong voice.

"It is foolish and wicked," he said unsteadily.

"Wish!" repeated his wife.

He raised his hand. "I wish my son alive again."

The paw fell to the floor where he looked at it, shuddering. Then he sank trembling into a chair as the old woman, with burning eyes, walked to the window and raised the blind.

He sat until he was chilled with the cold, glancing occasionally at the figure of the old woman peering through the window. The candle had burned below the rim of the china candlestick. It threw flickering shadows on the ceiling and walls, until, with a flicker larger than the rest, it went out. The old man felt unspeakably relieved that the charm had failed. He went back to bed, and a minute or two later the old woman lay silently beside him.

Neither spoke, but both lay listening to the ticking of the clock. A stair creaked, and a squeaky mouse scurried noisily through the wall. The darkness was unpleasant. After lying for some time trying to get up his courage, the husband took the box of matches, and striking one, went downstairs for a candle.

At the foot of the stairs the match went out, and he paused to strike another. At the same moment a knock, so quiet he barely heard it, sounded on the front door.

The matches fell from his hand. He stood motionless, not breathing until the knock was repeated. Then he turned and ran swiftly back to his room and closed the door behind him. A third knock sounded through the house.

"What's that?" cried the old woman, sitting up.

"A rat," said the old man, in shaking tones, "a rat. It passed me on the stairs."

His wife sat up in bed listening. A loud knock sounded through the house.

"It's Herbert!" she screamed. "It's Herbert!"

She ran to the door, but her husband was before her, and catching her by the arm, held her tightly.

"What are you going to do?" he whispered.

"It's my boy; it's Herbert!" she cried, struggling. "I forgot it was two miles away. What are you holding me for? Let go. I must open the door."

"For God's sake don't let it in," cried the old man trembling.

"You're afraid of your own son," she cried, struggling. "Let me go. I'm coming, Herbert; I'm coming."

There was another knock, and another. With a sudden movement, the old woman broke free and ran from the room. Her husband followed to the landing, and called her to come back as she hurried downstairs. He heard the chain rattle and the bolt at the bottom of the door drawn slowly and stiffly from the socket. Then the old woman's voice, strained and panting.

"The bolt," she cried loudly. "Come down. I can't reach it."

But her husband was on his hands and knees, reaching blindly about on the floor in search of the paw. If he could only find it before the thing outside got in. A long series of knocks echoed through the house, and he heard the scraping of a chair as his wife placed it against the door. He heard the creaking of the bolt as it came slowly back, and at the same moment, he found the monkey's paw, and frantically breathed his third and last wish.

The knocking stopped suddenly, although the echoes of it were still in the house. He heard the chair drawn back and the door opened. A cold wind rushed up the staircase. A long, loud wail of disappointment and misery from his wife gave him courage to run down to her side, and then to the gate outside. The streetlamp flickering opposite shone on a quiet and deserted road. ■

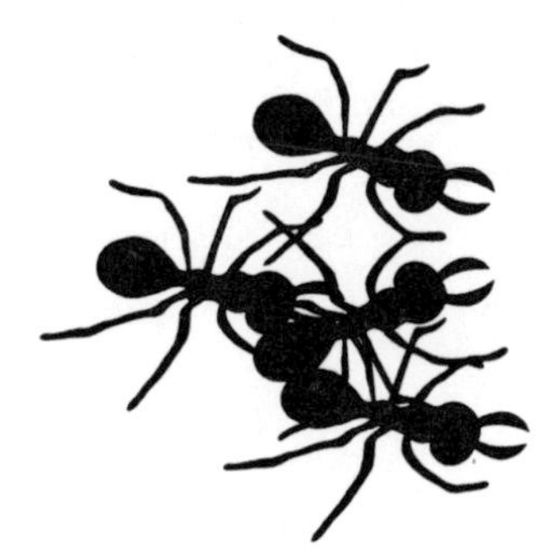

PREVIEW

To Leiningen, the owner of a plantation in Brazil, the human mind is the most powerful force on earth. But Leiningen is about to face an enemy whose own fierce intelligence is almost beyond imagining. In a gamble of life and death, Leiningen is about to find out whether reason is any match for Nature.

LEININGEN VERSUS THE ANTS

Carl Stephenson

"Unless they alter their course, and there's no reason why they should, they'll reach your plantation in two days at the latest."

Leiningen sucked calmly at a cigar about the size of a corncob, and, for a few seconds, gazed without answering at the worried District Commissioner. Then he took the cigar from his lips and leaned slightly forward. With his bristling gray hair, bulky nose, and intelligent eyes, he had the look of an aging and shabby eagle.

"Decent of you," he murmured, "paddling all this way just to give me the tip. But you're pulling my leg, of course, when you say I must run. Why, even a herd of dinosaurs couldn't drive me from this plantation of mine."

The Brazilian official threw up lean and lanky arms and clawed the air in frustration. "Leiningen!" he shouted. "You're insane! They're not creatures you can fight—they're an act of God! Ten miles long, two miles wide—ants, nothing but ants! And every single one of them a fiend from hell; before you can spit three times, they'll eat a full-grown buffalo to the bones. I tell you, if you don't clear out at once there'll be nothing left of you but a skeleton picked as clean as your own plantation."

Leiningen grinned. "Act of God, my eye! I'm not going to run for it just because an army of ants is on the way. And don't think I'm the kind of fathead who tries to fend off lightning with his fists, either. I use my intelligence, old man. I know what my brain is for. When I began this farm and plantation three years ago, I took into account all that could conceivably happen to it. And now I'm ready for anything and everything—including your ants."

The Brazilian rose heavily to his feet. "I've done my best," he gasped. "Your obstinacy endangers not only yourself, but the lives of your four hundred workers. You don't know these ants!"

Leiningen accompanied him down to the river, where the Government launch was moored. The vessel cast off. As it moved downstream, the official neared the rail and began waving his arms frantically. Long after the launch had disappeared round the bend, Leiningen thought he could still hear that imploring voice, "You don't know them, I tell you! You don't know them!"

But the reported enemy was by no means unfamiliar to the planter. Before he started work on his settlement, he had lived a long time in this country. He had seen for himself the fearful damage sometimes wrought by these ravenous insects in their campaigns for food. But since then he had planned his own measures of defense. These, he was convinced, were in every way adequate to withstand the approaching peril.

Moreover, during his three years as a planter, Leiningen had met and defeated drought, disease and all other "acts of God" which had come against him—unlike his fellow settlers in the district, who had made little or no resistance. This success he attributed to the observance of his lifelong motto: The human brain needs only to become fully aware of its powers to conquer even the elements. Dull people fell senselessly and needlessly into disaster; even bright-enough people lost their heads and ran into stone walls when circumstances suddenly altered or accelerated; the lazy drifted with the current until they were caught in whirlpools and dragged under. But such disasters, Leiningen claimed, merely strengthened his argument that intelligence, properly directed, always makes man the master of his fate.

Yes, Leiningen had always known how to grapple with life. Even here, in this Brazilian wilderness, his brain had triumphed over every difficulty and danger it had so far encountered. First he had vanquished primal forces by cunning and organization. Next he had enlisted the resources of modern science to increase miraculously the yield of his plantation. And now he was sure he would prove more than a match for the "irresistible" ants.

That same evening, however, Leiningen assembled his workers. He had no intention of waiting till the news reached their ears from other sources. Most of them had been born in the district; the cry "The ants are coming!" was to them a signal for instant, panic-stricken flight, a spring for life itself.

But his workers had learned to trust Leiningen's wisdom, and they heard his news calmly. They waited, unafraid, alert, as if for the beginning of a new game or hunt which he had just described to them. The ants were indeed mighty, but the brain of man was mightier. Let them come!

They came at noon the second day. Their approach was announced by the wild unrest of the horses, scarcely controllable now either in stall or under rider, scenting the coming horror.

It was announced by a stampede of animals, timid and savage, hurtling past each other. Jaguars and pumas flashed by the nimble stags of the pampas. Bulky tapirs, no longer hunters, themselves hunted, outpaced fleet antelope. Maddened herds of cattle, heads lowered, nostrils snorting, rushed through tribes of loping monkeys, chattering in crazed terror. Then followed the creeping and springing inhabitants of bush and field, big and little rodents, snakes, and lizards.

Pell-mell the rabble swarmed down the hill to the plantation. They scattered right and left before the barrier of the water-filled ditch, then sped onwards to the river. There, again hindered, they fled along its bank out of sight.

This water-filled ditch was one of the defense measures which Leiningen had prepared against the ants. It encompassed three sides of the plantation like a huge horseshoe. Twelve feet across, but not very deep, when dry it was hardly an obstacle to either man or beast. But the ends of the "horseshoe" ran into the river which formed the northern boundary—and fourth side—of the plantation. And at the end nearer the house and outbuildings in the middle of the plantation, Leiningen had constructed a dam. By means of the dam, water from the river could be diverted into the ditch.

So now, by opening the dam, he was able to fling an imposing wall of water, a huge rectangle with the river as its base, completely around the plantation, like the moat encircling a medieval city. Unless the ants were clever enough to build rafts, they had no hope of reaching the plantation, Leiningen concluded.

The twelve-foot water ditch seemed to afford all the security needed. But while waiting the arrival of the ants, Leiningen made a further improvement. The western section of the ditch ran along the edge of a forest, and the branches of some great trees reached over the water. Leiningen now had them chopped off so that ants could not descend from them within the "moat."

Finally, he made a careful inspection of the "inner moat"—a smaller ditch lined with concrete, which extended around the hill on which stood the ranch house, barns, stables, and other buildings. Into this concrete ditch emptied the inflow pipes from three great gasoline tanks. If by some miracle the ants managed to cross the water and reached the plantation, this wall of gasoline would be absolute protection for the people, their homes, and their animals. Such, at least, was Leiningen's opinion.

He stationed his men at irregular distances along the water ditch, the first line of defense. Then he lay down in his hammock and puffed drowsily away at his pipe until a worker came with the report that the ants had been observed far away in the South.

Leiningen mounted his horse, which at the feel of its master seemed to forget its uneasiness, and rode leisurely in the direction of the threatening offensive. The southern stretch of ditch—the upper side of the rectangle—was nearly three miles long. From its center one could survey the entire countryside. This was destined to be the scene of the outbreak of war between Leiningen's brain and twenty square miles of life-destroying ants.

It was a sight one could never forget. Over the range of hills, as far as eye could see, crept a darkening line, ever longer and broader, spreading across the slope from east to west. The line then moved downwards, downwards, uncannily swift, and all the green vegetation of that wide area was being mown as by a giant sickle. All that was left was that vast moving shadow, extending, deepening, and moving rapidly nearer.

When Leiningen's men, behind their barrier of water, saw the approach of the long-expected foe, they screamed insults in its direction. But as the distance began to lessen between the "sons of hell" and the water ditch, they fell silent. Before the advance of that awe-inspiring throng, their belief in the powers of the boss began to steadily dwindle.

Even Leiningen himself, who had ridden up just in time to strengthen his men's spirits with a display of unshakable calm, could not free himself from a qualm of uneasiness. There were thousands of millions of ravenous jaws bearing down upon him. Only a suddenly insignificant, narrow ditch lay between him and his men being gnawed to the bones "before you can spit three times."

Hadn't this brain for once taken on more

than it could manage? If the evil things decided to rush the ditch and fill it to the brim with their corpses, there'd still be more than enough to destroy every trace of that skull of his. The planter's chin jutted; they hadn't got him yet, and he'd see to it they never would. While he could think at all, he'd defy both death and the devil.

The hostile army was approaching in perfect formation. No human battalions, however well-drilled, could ever hope to rival the precision of that advance. Along a front that moved forward as uniformly as a straight line, the ants drew nearer and nearer to the water ditch. Then, when they learned through their scouts the nature of the watery obstacle, the two outlying wings of the army detached themselves from the main body and marched down the western and eastern sides of the ditch.

This maneuver took more than an hour to accomplish. No doubt the ants expected that at some point they would find a way to cross the water.

During this movement by the outlying wings, the army on the center and southern front remained still. The men at the plantation were therefore able to have a good look at them. Some of the workers believed they could see, too, the brilliant, cold eyes and the razor-edged jaws of this endless army.

It is not easy for the average person to imagine that an animal, not to mention an insect, can think. But now both the minds of Leiningen and of his workers began to stir with the unpleasant suspicion that inside every single one of those insects dwelt a thought. And that thought was: Ditch or no ditch, we'll get to your flesh!

Not until four o'clock did the wings reach the "horseshoe" ends of the ditch, only to find these ran into the great river. Through some kind of secret telegraphy, the report must then have flashed very swiftly indeed along the entire enemy line. And Leiningen, riding—no longer casually—along his side of the ditch, noticed by energetic and widespread movements of troops that for some unknown reason the news had its greatest effect on the southern front, where the main army was massed. Perhaps the failure to find a way over the ditch was persuading the ants to withdraw from the plantation in search of an easier target.

An immense flood of ants, about a hundred yards in width, was pouring in a glimmering black wave down the far slope of the ditch. Many thousands were already drowning in slowly moving water there, but they were followed by troop after troop, who clambered over their sinking comrades. They themselves served as dying bridges to the reserves hurrying on behind.

Great groups of ants were being carried away by the current into the middle of the ditch, where gradually they broke apart and then, exhausted by their struggles, vanished below the surface. Nevertheless, the wavering, floundering hundred-yard front was surely if slowly advancing towards the men on the other bank. Leiningen had been wrong when he supposed the enemy would first have to fill the ditch with their bodies before they could cross. Instead, they merely needed to act as steppingstones, as they swam and sank, to the hordes ever pressing onwards from behind.

Near Leiningen a few mounted foremen awaited his orders. He sent one to the site of the dam, with instructions to increase the speed and power of the water coursing through the ditch.

A second man was sent to the outbuildings to bring shovels and gasoline sprinklers. A third rode away to call to the site of the offensive all the remaining men, except those at the observation posts.

The ants were getting across far more

quickly than Leiningen would have thought possible. Pushed along by the mighty wave of bodies behind them, they struggled nearer and nearer to the inner bank. The momentum of the attack was so great that the gentle flow of the stream did nothing to stop them. Into the gap left by every submerging insect hastened forward a dozen more.

When reinforcements reached Leiningen, the invaders were halfway over. The planter had to admit to himself that it was only by a stroke of luck for him that the ants were attempting the crossing on a relatively short area. If they had simultaneously assaulted the entire length of the ditch, the outlook for the defenders would have been grim indeed.

Even as it was, it could hardly be described as rosy, though the planter acted quite unaware that death in a gruesome form was drawing closer and closer. As the war between his brain and the "act of God" reached its climax, the shadow of death began to lose its power for Leiningen. He began to feel like an athlete in a new Olympic game, a gigantic and thrilling contest, from which he was determined to emerge victor. His aura of confidence was so strong that his workmen forgot their own fear. Under his supervision, they began hurriedly digging up to the edge of the bank and throwing clods of earth and spadefuls of sand into the midst of the hostile army.

The gasoline sprinklers, formerly used to destroy pests on the plantation, were also brought into action. Streams of evil-smelling gas now soared and fell over an enemy already in disorder through the bombardment of earth and sand.

The ants responded to these vigorous and successful measures of defense by new offensive actions. Entire clumps of huddling insects began to roll down the opposite bank into the water. At the same time, Leiningen noticed that the ants were now attacking along an ever-widening front. As the numbers both of his men and his gasoline sprayers were severely limited, this extension of the line of battle was becoming an overwhelming danger.

To add to his difficulties, the very clods of earth they flung into that black floating carpet often whirled fragments toward the men's own side, and here and there dark ribbons of ants were already scrambling up the inner bank. True, wherever a man saw these, they could still be driven back into the water by spadefuls of earth or jets of gasoline. But the line of men was too sparse and scattered to hold off these landing parties at all points, and though the men worked madly, their plight became more dangerous by the moment.

One man struck with his shovel at an enemy clump, then did not draw it back quickly enough from the water. In a flash the wooden handle swarmed with upward scurrying insects. With a curse, he dropped the shovel into the ditch. Too late—they were already on his body, stinging with their paralyzing venom. Screaming, frantic with pain, the man danced and twirled like one possessed by evil spirits.

Realizing that another such attack might plunge his men into panic and destroy their morale, Leiningen roared in a bellow louder than the yells of the victim: "Into the gasoline, man! Put your arms in the gasoline!" The man heard; he stopped twirling, then tore off his shirt and plunged his arm and the ants hanging to it up to the shoulder in one of the large open barrels of gas. But even then the fierce jaws did not loosen; another man had to help him squash and remove each separate insect.

Distracted by the episode, some men had turned away from the ditch. And now cries of fury, a thudding of spades, and a wild trampling to and fro, showed that the ants had made full use of the interval, though luckily only a few had managed to get across. The men set to work again desperately with the shower of earth and sand. Meanwhile an old Indian, who acted as medicine man to the plantation workers, gave the bitten worker a drink he had prepared some hours before. He claimed it could dissolve and weaken the ants' venom.

Leiningen surveyed his position. An observer would have estimated the odds against him at a thousand to one. But then such an onlooker would have judged only by what he saw—the advance of countless battalions of ants against the useless efforts of a few defenders—and not by the unseen activity that can go on in a man's brain.

For Leiningen had not made a mistake when he decided he would fight one element with another. The water in the ditch was beginning to rise; the stronger damming of the river was making itself felt.

Visibly the swiftness and power of the water increased. It swirled its living black surface into quicker and quicker movement, carrying away more and more of the ants on the hastening current.

Victory had been snatched from the very

jaws of defeat. With a hysterical shout of joy, the men feverishly intensified their bombardment of earth clods and sand.

And now the wide black flood of ants down the opposite bank was thinning and ceasing, as if the ants were becoming aware that they could not attain their aim. They were scurrying back up the slope to safety.

All the ant-troops so far hurled into the ditch had been sacrificed in vain. Drowned and floundering insects drifted in thousands along the flow, while Indians running on the bank destroyed every swimmer that reached the side.

Not until the ditch curved towards the east did the scattered ranks assemble again in organized fashion. And now, exhausted and half-numbed, they were in no condition to climb the bank. The shower of earth clods drove them round the bend towards the mouth of the ditch and then into the river, wherein they vanished without leaving a trace.

The news ran swiftly along the entire chain of outposts, and soon a long scattered line of laughing men could be seen hastening along the ditch towards the scene of victory.

Their former fear had vanished, and they now celebrated their victory wildly, as if there were no longer thousands of millions of merciless, cold and hungry eyes watching them from the opposite bank, watching and waiting.

The sun sank behind the rim of the forest and twilight deepened into night. It was not only hoped but expected that the ants would remain quiet until dawn. But to defeat any attempt at a crossing, the flow of water through the ditch was powerfully increased by opening the dam still further.

In spite of this barrier, Leiningen was not yet altogether convinced that the ants would not try another surprise attack. He ordered his men to camp along the bank overnight. He also sent parties of them to patrol the ditch in two of his motor cars. He instructed them to constantly illuminate the surface of the water with headlights and flashlights.

After having taken all the precautions he deemed necessary, Leiningen ate his supper with considerable appetite and went to bed. His slumbers were peaceful, undisturbed by the memory of the waiting, live, twenty square miles.

Dawn found a thoroughly refreshed and active Leiningen riding along the edge of the ditch. The planter saw before him a motionless and unaltered throng of ants. He studied the wide belt of water between them and the plantation, and for a moment almost regretted that the fight had ended so soon and so simply. In the comforting, matter-of-fact light of morning, it seemed to him now that the ants hadn't the ghost of a chance to cross the ditch. Even if they plunged headlong into it on all three fronts at once, the force of the now powerful current would inevitably sweep them away. He had got quite a thrill out of the fight—a pity it was already over.

He rode along the eastern and southern sections of the ditch and found everything in order. Then he reached the western section, opposite the forest. Here, contrary to the other battle fronts, he found the enemy very busy indeed. The trunks and branches of the trees fairly swarmed with industrious insects. But instead of eating the leaves there and then, they were merely gnawing through the stalks, so that a thick green shower fell steadily to the ground.

No doubt they had been sent out to obtain food for the rest of the army. The discovery did not surprise Leiningen. He did not need to be told that ants are intelligent, that certain species even use others as milk cows, watchdogs, and slaves. He was well aware of their power of adaptation, their sense of discipline, their marvelous talent for organization.

His belief that this was a food-gathering mission was strengthened when he saw the leaves that fell to the ground being dragged to the troops waiting outside the wood. Then all at once he realized the aim that rain of green was intended to serve.

Each single leaf, pulled or pushed by dozens of toiling insects, was borne straight to the edge of the ditch. Leiningen saw the woods move nearer and nearer in the jaws of the ants. Watching this development, he was forced to admit to himself that the situation was far more ominous than that of the day before.

He had thought it impossible for the ants to build rafts for themselves. Well, here they were, coming in thousands, more than enough to bridge the ditch. Leaves after leaves rustled down the slope into the water, where the current drew them away from the bank and carried them into midstream. And every single leaf carried several ants. This time the farmer did not trust to the speed of his messengers. He galloped away, leaning from his saddle and yelling orders as he rushed past outpost after outpost: "Bring gasoline pumps to the southwest front! Issue shovels to every man along the line facing the wood!" And when he arrived at the eastern and southern sections, he sent every man except the observation posts to the menaced west.

Then, as he rode past the stretch where the ants had failed to cross the day before, he witnessed a brief but impressive scene. Down the slope of the distant hill there came towards him a strange creature, writhing rather than running, an animal-like blackened statue with shapeless head and four quivering feet that buckled under it almost constantly. When the creature reached the far bank of the ditch and collapsed opposite Leiningen, he recognized it as a stag, covered over and over with ants.

It had strayed near the zone of the army. As usual, they had attacked its eyes first. Blinded, it had reeled in the madness of hideous torment straight into the ranks of its persecutors, and now the beast swayed to and fro in its death agony.

With a shot from his rifle Leiningen put it out of its misery. Then he pulled out his watch. He knew he hadn't a second to lose. But for life itself, he could not have denied his curiosity the satisfaction of knowing how long the ants would take—for personal reasons, so to speak. After six minutes the white polished bones alone remained. That's how he himself could look—Leiningen spat once and put spurs to his horse.

The sporting spirit which the contest had inspired in him the day before had now vanished. In its place was a cold and violent purpose. He would send these vermin back to the hell where they belonged, somehow, anyhow. Yes, but "how" was indeed the question. As things stood at present, it looked as if the devils would erase him and his men from the earth instead. He had underestimated the might of the enemy. It would be hard work indeed to outwit them.

The biggest danger now, he decided, was the point where the western section of the ditch curved southwards. And when he arrived there, he found his worst expectations were justified. The power of the current had brought the leaves and their crews of ants so close together at the bend that their bridge was almost created.

True, streams of gasoline and clumps of earth still prevented a landing. But the number of floating leaves was increasing ever more swiftly. It could not be long now before a stretch of water a mile long was covered by a green walkway over which the ants could rush in millions.

Leiningen galloped to the site of the dam. The damming of the river was controlled by a wheel on its bank. The planter ordered the man at the wheel first to lower the water in the ditch almost to vanishing point, next to wait a moment, then suddenly to let the river in again. This maneuver of lowering and raising the surface, of decreasing, then increasing the flow of water through the ditch, was to be repeated over and over again until further notice.

This tactic was at first successful. The water in the ditch sank, and with it the film of leaves. The green fleet nearly reached the bed of the ditch, and the troops on the far bank swarmed down the slope to it. Then a violent flow of water raced through the ditch, overwhelming leaves and ants, and sweeping them along.

This repeated, rapid flushing prevented just in time the almost completed crossing of the ditch. But it also flung here and there squads of the enemy up the inner bank. These seemed to know their duty only too well, and lost no time accomplishing it. The air rang with the curses of bitten men. They had removed their shirts and pants to detect more quickly the upwards-hastening insects; when they saw one, they crushed it.

Fortunately the attack as yet was only by a few ants. Again and again, the water sank and rose, carrying leaves and drowned ants away with it. It lowered once more nearly to its bed; but this time the exhausted defenders waited in vain for the flush of destruction. Leiningen sensed disaster; something must have gone wrong with the machinery of the dam. Then a sweating workman raced up to him—

"They're over!"

While the men were concentrating upon the defense of the stretch opposite the wood, the seemingly unaffected line beyond the wood had become the place of decisive action. Here the men were sparse and scattered; everyone who could be spared had hurried away to the south.

Just as the man at the dam had lowered the water almost to the bed of the ditch, the ants on a wide front began another attempt at a direct crossing like that of the preceding day. Into the emptied bed poured an irresistible throng. Rushing across the ditch, they attained the inner bank before the men fully grasped the situation. Their frantic screams dumbfounded the man at the controls of the dam. Before he could turn the wheel again to raise the water level, he saw himself surrounded by raging ants. He ran like the others, ran for his life.

When Leiningen heard this, he knew the plantation was doomed. He wasted no time bemoaning the fact. For as long as there was the slightest chance of success, he had stood his ground, and now any further resistance was both useless and dangerous. He fired three revolver shots into the air—the prearranged signal for his men to retreat instantly within the "inner moat." Then he rode toward the ranch house.

This was two miles from the point of invasion. There was therefore time enough to prepare the second line of defense against the advent of the ants. Of the three great gasoline tanks near the house, one had already been half emptied by the constant withdrawals needed for the pumps during the fight at the water ditch. The remaining gas in it was now drawn off through underground pipes into the concrete trench which encircled the ranch house and its outbuildings.

And there, in twos and threes, Leiningen's men reached him. Most of them were obviously trying to preserve an air of calm and indifference, but their restless glances and worried brows showed their true frames of mind. One could see their belief in a victory was considerably shaken.

The planter called his workers around him.

"Well, lads," he began, "we've lost the first round. But we'll smash the beggars yet, don't you worry. Anyone who thinks otherwise can take his pay here and now and push off. There are rafts enough to spare on the river and plenty of time still to reach 'em."

Not a man stirred.

Leiningen acknowledged this silent vote of confidence with a laugh that was half a grunt. "That's the stuff, lads. It'd be too bad to miss the rest of the show, eh? Well, the fun won't start till morning. Once these blighters turn tail, there'll be plenty of work for everyone and higher wages all round. And now run along and get something to eat; you've earned it all right."

In the excitement of the fight the greater part of the day had passed without the men once pausing to snatch a bite. Now that the ants were for the time being out of sight, and the wall of gasoline gave a stronger feeling of security, hungry stomachs began to assert their claims.

The bridges over the concrete ditch were removed. Here and there solitary ants had reached the ditch; they gazed at the gasoline thoughtfully, then scurried back again. Apparently they had little interest at the moment for what lay beyond the evil-smelling barrier. The abundant food of the plantation was the main attraction. Soon the trees, shrubs and beds for miles around were covered with ants zealously gobbling the crops raised over long weary months of toil.

As twilight began to fall, a column of ants marched around the gasoline trench, but as yet made no move towards its edge. Leiningen posted sentries with headlights and flashlights, then withdrew to his office and began to reckon up his losses. He estimated these as large, but, in comparison with his bank balance, they were not unbearable. He worked out in detail a plan of intensive farming which would enable him, before very long, to compensate himself for the damage now being wrought to his crops. It was with a contented mind that he finally went himself to bed. There he slept deeply until dawn, undisturbed by any thought that the next day little more might be left of him than a glistening skeleton.

He rose with the sun and went out on the flat roof of his house. And a scene like one from Hell itself lay around him. For miles in every direction there was nothing but a black, glittering multitude, a multitude of rested, well-fed, but none the less aggressive ants. Yes, look as far as one might, one could see nothing but that rustling black throng, except in the north, where the great river drew a boundary they could not hope to pass. But even the high stone breakwater along the bank of the river, was, like the paths, the shorn trees and shrubs, the ground itself, black with ants.

So their greed was not satisfied in razing that vast plantation? Not by a long shot. They seemed all the more eager now to claim a rich treasure: four hundred men, numerous horses, and bursting granaries.

At first it seemed that the gasoline trench would serve its purpose. The ants sensed the danger of swimming it, and made no move to plunge blindly over its brink. Instead they devised a better plan. They began to collect shreds of bark, twigs and dried leaves and dropped these into the gasoline. Everything green, which could have been similarly used, had long since been eaten. After a time, though, a long procession could be seen bringing from the west the leaves used as rafts the day before.

Since the gasoline, unlike the water in the outer ditch, was perfectly still, the twigs and leaves stayed where they were thrown. It was several hours before the ants succeeded in covering an appreciable part of the surface. At length, however, they were ready to proceed to a direct attack.

Their storm troops swarmed down the concrete side, scrambled over the supporting surface of twigs and leaves, and ferried their rafts over the few remaining streaks of open gasoline until they reached the other side. Then they began to climb up this to make straight for the helpless men.

During the entire offensive, the planter sat peacefully, watching them with interest, but not stirring a muscle. Moreover, he had ordered his men not to disturb in any way the advancing horde. So they sat along the bank of the ditch and waited for a sign from the boss. The gasoline was now covered with ants. A few had climbed the inner concrete wall and were scurrying towards the defenders.

"Everyone back from the ditch!" roared Leiningen. The men rushed away, without the slightest idea of his plan. He stooped forward and cautiously dropped into the ditch a stone. It split the floating carpet and its living freight, to reveal a gleaming patch of gasoline. A match spurted, sank down to the oily surface—Leiningen sprang back. In a flash a towering wall of fire encompassed the settlement.

This spectacular display delighted the men. They applauded, yelled, and stamped with approval.

It was some time before the gasoline burned down to the bed of the ditch, and the wall of smoke and flame began to lower. The ants had retreated in a wide circle from the devastation. Innumerable charred fragments along the outer bank showed that the flames had spread from the fire in the ditch well into the ranks of ants, where they had spread death far and wide.

Yet the perseverance of the ants was by no means broken. Indeed, each setback seemed only to strengthen it. The concrete cooled, the flicker of the dying flames wavered and vanished, gasoline from the second tank was poured into the trench—and the ants marched forward to renew the attack.

The foregoing scene repeated itself in every detail, except that on this occasion the ants needed less time to bridge the ditch, for the gasoline was already filmed by a layer of ash. Once again they withdrew; once again gas flowed into the ditch. Would the creatures never learn that their self-sacrifice was utterly senseless? It really was senseless, wasn't it? Yes, of course it was senseless—provided the defenders had a limitless supply of gasoline.

When Leiningen reached this stage of reasoning, he felt for the first time since the arrival of the ants that his confidence was deserting him. His skin began to creep; he loosened his collar. Once the devils were over the trench, there wasn't a chance in hell for him and his men. God, what a prospect, to be eaten alive like that!

For the third time, the flames enveloped the attacking troops and burned down to extinction. Yet the ants were coming on again as if nothing had happened. And meanwhile Leiningen had made a discovery that chilled him to the bone: Gasoline was no longer flowing into the ditch. Something must be blocking the outflow pipe of the third and last tank. What was it—a snake or a dead rat? Whatever it was, the ants could be held off no longer, unless gasoline could somehow be led from the tank into the ditch.

Then Leiningen remembered that in an outhouse nearby were two old disused fire engines. Moving faster than they ever had in their lives, the workmen dragged them out of the shed, connected their pumps to the tank, uncoiled and laid the hose. They were just in time to aim a stream of gas at a column of ants that had already crossed and drive them back down the incline into the ditch. Once more an oily barrier surrounded the settlement; once more it was possible to hold the position—for the moment.

It was obvious, however, that this last resource meant only the postponement of defeat and death. A few of the workmen fell on their knees and began to pray. Others, shrieking insanely, fired their revolvers at the black, advancing masses, as if they felt their despair was pitiful enough to sway fate itself to mercy.

At length, two of the workers' nerves broke: Leiningen saw one naked man leap over the north side of the gasoline trench, quickly followed by a second. They sprinted with incredible speed towards the river. But their fleetness did not save them; long before they could reach the rafts, the enemy covered their bodies from head to foot.

In the agony of their torment, both sprang blindly into the wide river, where enemies no less sinister awaited them. Wild screams of mortal anguish informed the breathless onlookers that crocodiles and sword-toothed piranhas were no less ravenous than ants, and even quicker in reaching their prey.

In spite of this bloody warning, more and more men showed they were making up their minds to run the blockade. Anything, even a fight midstream against alligators, seemed better than powerlessly waiting for death to come and slowly consume their living bodies.

Leiningen flogged his brain till it reeled. Was there nothing on earth that could sweep this devil's spawn back into the hell from which it came?

Then out of the inferno of his bewilderment rose a terrifying inspiration. Yes, one hope remained, and one alone. It might be possible to dam the great river completely, so that its waters would fill not only the water ditch but overflow into the entire gigantic "saucer" of land in which lay the plantation.

The far bank of the river was too high for the waters to escape that way. The stone breakwater ran between the river and the plantation; its only gaps occurred where the "horseshoe" ends of the water ditch passed into the river. So its waters would not only be forced to inundate the plantation; they would also be held there by the breakwater until they rose to its own high level. In half an hour, perhaps even sooner, the plantation and its hostile army of occupation would be flooded.

The ranch house and outbuildings stood upon rising ground. Their foundations were higher than the breakwater, so the flood would not reach them. And any remaining ants trying to ascend the slope could be repulsed by gasoline.

It was possible—yes, if one could only get to the dam! A distance of nearly two miles lay between the ranch house and the dam—two miles of ants. Those two workmen had managed only a fifth of that distance at the cost of their lives. Was there another man he could ask to run five times as far? Hardly likely; and if there were, his prospect of getting back was almost zero.

No, there was only one thing for it, he'd have to make the attempt himself. He might as well be running as sitting still, anyway, when the ants finally got him. Besides, there was a bit of a chance. Perhaps the ants weren't so almighty, after all; perhaps he had allowed the mass suggestion of that evil black throng to hypnotize him, just as a snake fascinates and overpowers.

The ants were building their bridges. Leiningen got up on a chair. "Hey, lads, listen to me!" he cried. Slowly and listlessly, from all sides of the trench, the men began to shuffle towards him, the apathy of death already stamped on their faces.

"Listen, lads!" he shouted. "I'm proud of all you've done, and there's still a chance to save our lives—by flooding the plantation from the river. Now one of you might manage to get as far as the dam—but he'd never come back. Well, I'm not going to let you try it; if I did I'd be worse than one of those ants. No, I called the tune, and now I'm going to pay the piper.

"The moment I'm over the ditch, set fire to the gasoline. That'll allow time for the flood to do the trick. Then all you have to do is wait here all snug and quiet till I'm back. Yes, I'm coming back, trust me"—he grinned—"when I've finished my weight-loss workout."

He pulled on high leather boots, drew heavy gloves over his hands, and stuffed the spaces between trousers and boots, gloves and arms, shirt and neck, with rags soaked in gasoline. With close-fitting mosquito goggles he shielded his eyes, knowing too well the ants' trick of first robbing their victim of sight. Finally, he plugged his nostrils and ears with cotton-wool and let the men drench his clothes with gasoline.

He was about to set off, when the old Indian medicine man came up to him. He had a wondrous medicine, he said, prepared from a species of beetle whose odor was intolerable to ants. Yes, this odor protected these beetles from the attacks of even the most murderous ants. The Indian smeared the boss' boots, his gloves, and his face over and over with the extract.

Leiningen then remembered the paralyzing effect of ants' venom, and the Indian gave him a gourd full of the medicine he had administered to the bitten workman at the water ditch. The planter drank it down without noticing its bitter taste; his mind was already at the dam.

He started off towards the northwest corner of the trench. With a bound he was over—and among the ants.

The beleaguered men left behind had no opportunity to watch Leiningen's race against death. The ants were climbing the inner bank again—the lurid ring of gasoline blazed high. For the fourth time that day, the reflection from the fire shone on the sweating faces of the imprisoned men and on the reddish-black jaws of their attackers. The red and blue dark-edged flames leaped vividly now, celebrating what? The funeral pyre of the four hundred men, or of the hosts of attacking ants? Leiningen ran. He ran in long, equal strides, with only one thought, one sensation, in his being—he must get through. He dodged all trees and shrubs; except for the split seconds his soles touched the ground, the ants should have no opportunity to light on him. That they would get to him soon, despite the salve on his boots, the gasoline in his clothes, he realized only too well, but he knew even more surely that he must, and that he would, get to the dam.

Apparently the salve was some use after all; not until he reached halfway did he feel ants under his clothes, and a few on his face. Mechanically, not pausing, he struck at them, scarcely conscious of their bites. He saw he was drawing appreciably nearer the dam—the distance grew less and less—sank to five hundred—three—two—one hundred yards.

Then he was at the dam and gripping the ant-covered wheel. Hardly had he seized it when a horde of infuriated ants flowed over his hands, arms and shoulders. He started the wheel—before it turned once on its axis the swarm covered his face. Leiningen strained like a madman, his lips pressed tight; if he opened them to draw breath . . .

He turned and turned; slowly the dam lowered until it reached the bed of the river. Already the water was overflowing the ditch.

Another minute, and the river was pouring through the nearby gap in the breakwater. The flooding of the plantation had begun.

Leiningen let go of the wheel. Now, for the first time, he realized he was coated from head to foot with a layer of ants. In spite of the gasoline, his clothes were full of them. Several had got to his body or were clinging to his face. Now that he had completed his task, he felt the smart raging over his flesh from the bites of sawing and piercing insects.

Frantic with pain, he almost plunged into the river. To be ripped and splashed to shreds by piranhas? Already he was running the return journey, knocking ants from his gloves and jacket, brushing them from his bloodied face, squashing them to death under his clothes.

One of the creatures bit him just below the rim of his goggles; he managed to tear it away, but the agony of the bite and its etching acid drilled into the eye nerves. He saw now through circles of fire into a milky mist, then he ran for a time almost blinded, knowing that if he once tripped and fell. . . . The medicine man's brew didn't seem much good; it weakened the poison a bit, but didn't get rid of it. His heart pounded as if it would burst; blood roared in his ears; a giant's fist battered his lungs.

Then he could see again, but the burning wall of gasoline appeared infinitely far away; he could not last half that distance. Swift-changing pictures flashed through his head, episodes in his life. In another part of his brain, a cool and impartial onlooker informed this ant-blurred, gasping, exhausted bundle named Leiningen that such a rushing confusion of scenes from one's past is seen only in the moment before death.

A stone in the path . . . too weak to avoid it . . . the planter stumbled and collapsed. He tried to rise . . . he must be pinned under a rock . . . it was impossible . . . the slightest movement was impossible . . .

Then all at once, starkly clear and huge, and, right before his eyes, furred with ants, towering and swaying in its death agony, the stag appeared. In six minutes—gnawed to the bones. God, he couldn't die like that! And something outside him seemed to drag him to his feet. He tottered. He began to stagger forward again.

Through the blazing ring hurtled a vision which, as soon as it reached the ground on the inner side, fell full length and did not move. Leiningen, at the moment he made that leap through the flames, lost consciousness for the first time in his life. As he lay there, with glazing eyes and ripped face, he appeared a man returned from the grave. The workmen rushed to him, stripped off his clothes, tore away the ants from a body that seemed almost one open wound; in some paces the bones were showing. They carried him into the ranch house.

As the curtain of flames lowered, one could see in place of the uncountable host of ants an extensive vista of water. The dammed river had swept over the plantation, carrying with it the entire army. The water had collected and mounted in the great "saucer," while the ants had in vain attempted to reach the hill on which stood the ranch house. The belt of flames held them back.

And so imprisoned between water and fire, they had been delivered into the destruction that was their god. And near the farther mouth of the water ditch, where the stone breakwater had its second gap, the ocean swept the lost battalions into the river, to vanish forever.

The ring of fire dwindled as the water rose and quenched the dimming flames. The water climbed higher and higher. Because its outflow was slowed by the timber and underbrush it had carried along with it, its surface required some time to reach the top of the high stone breakwater and discharge over it the rest of the shattered army.

It swelled over shrubs and bushes, until it washed against the foot of the knoll on which the besieged men had taken refuge. For a while an army of ants tried again and again to attain this dry land, only to be repulsed by streams of gasoline back into the merciless flood.

Leiningen lay on his bed, his body bound from head to foot in bandages. With drugs and salves, they had managed to stop the bleeding and had dressed his many wounds. Now they thronged around him, one question in every face. Would he recover? "He won't die," said the old man who had bandaged him, "if he doesn't want to."

The planter opened his eyes. "Everything in order?" he asked.

"They're gone," said his nurse. "To hell." He held out a gourd full of a powerful sleeping medicine. Leiningen gulped it down.

"I told you I'd come back," he murmured, "even if I am a bit slimmed down." He grinned and shut his eyes. He slept. ■

PREVIEW

Once upon a time, there was a poor but honest young man who loved the daughter of a king . .

Who can count how many stories have begun with this idea? But mong them all, the story that follows stands alone. Its mixture of comedy, tragedy, suspense, and surprise has made "The Lady, or the Tiger?" unforgettable for generations of readers.

THE LADY, OR THE TIGER?

Frank R. Stockton

In the old, old days there lived a semi-savage king. His ideas were somewhat tamed by his living near more civilized neighbors, but they were still flashy and outlandish. He was a man of wild imagination, and he was so sure of himself that he could easily turn his opinions into facts. He often talked to himself, and once he and himself agreed on anything, the thing was done. When the people around him acted as he wanted them to, he was friendly and pleasant. And when they did not act as he wanted, he became even more friendly and pleasant, because nothing pleased him so much as to crush the misbehavior out of them.

One of the ideas that he had borrowed from his civilized neighbors was that of the arena, an area for public amusement. There his subjects could watch displays of human and animal bravery. This, he supposed, would teach and entertain his people.

But even here the wild savage imagination got the upper hand. The arena of the king was not built, as you might think, so that the people could hear the brave final words of dying gladiators, or watch the fate of the religiously opinionated as they were thrown to the lions. No, the huge arena was a place of justice, in which crime was punished and virtue rewarded—all through the hand of chance.

When a subject was accused of a crime that was important enough to interest the king, it was announced that on a certain day the fate of the accused person would be decided in the king's arena.

When all the people had gathered in the galleries that circled the arena, and the king sat high up on his throne, he gave a signal. Immediately a door beneath him opened, and the accused subject stepped out into the arena. Directly opposite him, on the other side of the enclosed space, were two doors. The doors were exactly alike. The duty of the person on trial was to walk directly to these doors and open one of them. He could open either door he pleased. Nothing but the purest chance would guide him. If he opened one, there came out of it a hungry tiger, the fiercest and most cruel that could be found. The tiger immediately sprang upon him and tore him to pieces as a punishment for his guilt. The moment this happened, iron bells were rung and great wails went up from the hired mourners. Then the huge audience, with bowed heads and downcast hearts, trudged slowly to their homes. They mourned that one so young and fair, or so old and respected, should have met such an awful fate.

But if the accused person opened the other door, there came forth from it a lady. She had been chosen as the most perfect match possible for the accused man. To this lady he was immediately married, as a reward for his innocence. It did not matter that he might already have a wife, or that he might be in love with someone he himself had chosen. Such unimportant matters could not interfere with the king's great plan of punishment and reward. As in the case of the punishment, the reward took place immediately. Another door opened beneath the king. From there a priest came out, followed by a choir of singers and dancing maidens playing joyous songs on golden horns. The wedding was promptly performed. Then the happy brass bells rang, the people shouted glad hurrahs, and the innocent man, with children strewing flowers on his path, led his bride home.

This was the king's semi-savage method of doing justice. Its perfect fairness is obvious. The criminal could not know out of which door would come the lady. He opened either door he pleased, without having the slightest idea whether he was to be eaten or married. Sometimes the tiger came out of one door, and sometimes out of the other. The accused person was instantly punished if he found himself guilty. If he was innocent, he was rewarded on the spot, whether he liked it or not. There was no escape from the judgments of the king's arena.

The arena was a very popular place. When the people gathered together on one of the great trial days, they never knew whether they were to witness a bloody slaughter or a joyous wedding. This uncertainty was highly exciting. The people were entertained and pleased. And no one could accuse the plan of being unfair, for didn't the accused person have the whole matter in his own hands?

This semi-savage king had a daughter as lovely as he could imagine, and with a soul as fiery and strong-willed as his own. As is usual in such cases, she was the apple of his eye, and was loved by him above all humanity. And there was a young man who was as pure of heart, and as poor of pocketbook, as is usually the case among young men who love royal maidens. This royal maiden was well satisfied with her lover, for he was more handsome and brave than any other man in the kingdom. This love affair moved on happily for many months, until one day the king happened to discover its existence. He did not hesitate. The youth was immediately thrown into prison, and a day was set for his trial in the king's arena. This, of course, was an especially important occasion. His majesty, as well as all the people, was greatly interested in what would happen. Never before had such a case occurred. Never before had a subject dared to love the daughter of the king.

The tiger-cages of the kingdom were searched for the most cruel and terrible beasts, from which the fiercest of all might be selected. At the same time, all the young women throughout the land were considered so that the young man might have a suitable bride, if that should be his fate. Of course, everybody knew that he was, in fact, guilty of what he was accused. He had loved the princess, and no one would deny it. But the king would not let any such fact interfere with his system of justice, in which he took such great delight. No matter how the affair turned out, the youth would be gotten rid of.

The appointed day arrived. From far and near the people gathered and crowded into the great galleries of the arena. Even more people, unable to fit in the galleries, waited outside. The king was in his place, opposite the twin doors, so terrible in their similarity.

All was ready. The signal was given. A door beneath the royal party opened, and the lover of the princess walked into the arena. His appearance was greeted with a low hum of admiration and anxiety. He was so tall, beautiful, and fair! Half the audience had not known so grand a youth had lived among them. No wonder the princess loved him! What a terrible thing for him to be there!

As the youth advanced into the arena, he turned, as the custom was, to bow to the king. But he was not thinking of the king. His eyes went straight to the princess, who sat to the right of her father. Had she not been semi-savage herself, she probably would not have been there. But her hotly burning nature would not allow her to miss an event in which she was so terribly interested. From the moment she had learned that her lover would be sent to the arena, she had thought of nothing else, night or day. The princess had more power and influence than anyone who had ever been interested in such a case. And as a result, she had done what no other person had done before: She had learned the secret of the doors. She knew in which of the rooms behind those doors stood the tiger, and in which waited the lady. Those rooms were thickly padded, so that no noise could give a hint to the person standing before them. But gold, and the power of a woman's will, had brought the secret to the princess.

And not only did she know in which room stood the lady, all blushing and radiant. She also knew who the lady was. It was one of the loveliest of the young women of the court, and the princess hated her. Often had she seen, or imagined that she had seen, this fair creature looking admiringly at her lover. And sometimes she thought that he noticed those looks, and even returned them. Now and then she had seen them talking together.

It was only for a moment or two, but much can be said in a brief space. It may have been on most unimportant topics, but how could she know that? The girl was lovely, but she had dared to raise her eyes to the loved one of the princess. And so, with all the heat of her entirely savage ancestors, the princess hated the woman who blushed and trembled behind that silent door.

When her lover turned and looked at her, he saw, in the mysterious way that lovers know such things, that she knew the secret. He had expected her to know it. He understood her nature and had been sure she would never rest until she knew.

Then it was that his anxious glance asked the question: "Which?" It was as plain to her as if he shouted it from where he stood. There was not an instant to be lost. The question was asked in a flash; it must be answered in another.

Her right arm lay on the cushioned railing before her. She raised her hand, and made a slight, quick movement toward the right. No one but her lover saw her. Every eye but his was fixed on the man in the arena.

He turned, and with a firm and rapid step he walked across the empty space. Every heart stopped beating, every breath was held, every eye was fixed upon that man. Without the slightest hesitation, he went to the door on the right and opened it.

Now, the point of the story is this: Did the tiger come out of that door, or did the lady?

The more we think about this question, the harder it is to answer. It requires a study of the human heart and the twisted ways of passion, in which it is so easy to become lost. Think of it, dear reader, not as if you had made the decision. Think instead about that hot-blooded, semi-savage princess, her soul burning with the fires of despair and jealousy. She had lost him, but who should have him?

How often, in her waking hours and in her dreams, had she leaped up in wild horror and covered her face with her hands as she thought of her lover opening the door and meeting the cruel fangs of the tiger!

But how much oftener had she seen him at the other door! How she had ground her teeth, and torn her hair, when she imagined his delight as he opened the door of the lady! How her soul had burned in agony when she had seen him rush to meet that woman; when she had seen him lead her forth, glowing with the joy of recovered life; when she had heard the glad shouts from the crowd, and the wild ringing of the happy bells; when she had seen the priest make them man and wife before her very eyes; and when she had seen them walk away together upon their path of flowers, followed by the shouts of the happy crowd, in which her one despairing shriek was lost and drowned!

Wouldn't it be better for him to die at once, and go to wait for her in the blessed lands of a semi-savage paradise?

And yet, that awful tiger, those shrieks, that blood!

To him, she had indicated her decision in an instant. But it had been made after days and nights of tortured thought. She had known he would ask her. She had decided what she would answer. And, without the slightest hesitation, she had moved her hand to the right.

The question of her decision is one not to be easily decided. And I do not dare set myself up as the one person able to answer it. And so I leave it with all of you: Which came out of the opened door—the lady, or the tiger? ■

PREVIEW

Fifty below zero is no weather for a man to walk in. The dog in "To Build a Fire" knows this, but the man whom he follows does not. He reasons that he can outwit the forces of nature. The dog does not reason; still, he is wiser than the man. The man's gradual realization of his mistake gives "To Build a Fire" its slowly building sense of danger.

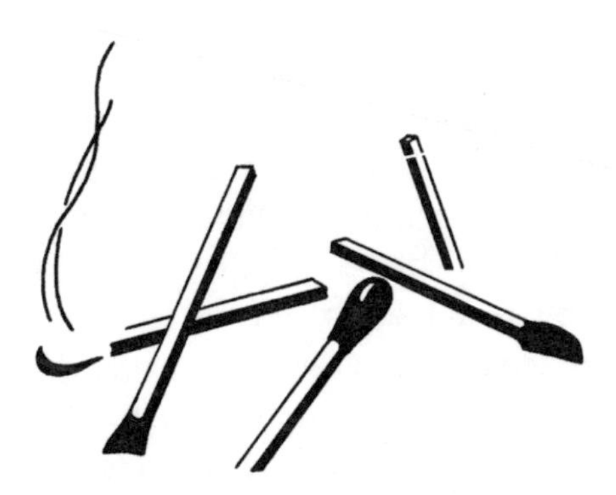

TO BUILD A FIRE

Jack London

Day had broken cold and gray, exceedingly cold and gray. The man turned away from the main Yukon trail and climbed a hill from where he spotted a little-traveled trail. He paused at the top of the hill and looked at his watch. It was nine o'clock. It was a clear day—there was no sun and not a cloud in the sky. He felt a subtle sense of gloom caused by the lack of sun. But this did not worry him. It had been days since he had seen the sun. He was used to lack of sun, and he knew that more days would pass before the sun would be in view again.

The man paused and looked around. The Yukon River was a mile wide and hidden under three feet of ice. On top of the ice were three feet of snow—all pure white. As far as the eye could see, the landscape was pure, unbroken white, except for a dark hairline that curved and twisted both to the south and to the north. This dark hairline was actually the main trail that went on for miles and miles—hundreds of miles to the south, and thousands of miles to the north.

But all of this . . . the far-reaching trail, the absence of sun in the sky, the tremendous cold and the strangeness of it all, made no impression on this man. You would think it would have. He was a newcomer to this land, and this was his first winter. But the trouble was that he had no imagination. He was quick and alert in dealing with actual things in life, but he did not see below the surface. He did not understand the meaning of things—for instance, that a temperature of fifty degrees below zero actually felt much, much colder. He understood only that this was cold and he was uncomfortable, but that was all. He did not think about the significance of the temperature. That a man could only live within a range of certain temperatures. That there were limits as to how much cold or heat a man could endure. He did not think in terms of life and death. Fifty degrees below just meant to him the need to wear mittens, ear flaps, thick socks and warm moccasins to protect against the hurt of frostbite. He didn't think beyond the basics of plain being cold. Nothing more entered his mind.

As he got ready to walk on, he spat. There was a sharp, explosive, crackling sound. He spat again. He was startled to find that the spittle froze in the air before it even reached the ground. From this he knew it was colder than fifty below zero—exactly how much, he didn't know. And it didn't matter to him. He was on his way to meet his friends at a place along Henderson Creek. He would reach their camp by six p.m. He knew his friends would be waiting. There would be a fire blazing, and a hot supper would be ready.

Then he thought about his lunch. He had biscuits bundled up in a handkerchief and stored beneath his jacket next to his bare skin. This was the only way to keep them from freezing. He smiled to himself, thinking of these biscuits, each enclosing a big slice of bacon.

He started to walk on through the big spruce trees. It was hard to even see the trail. A foot of snow had fallen since the last sled had gone by. But he was glad he was on foot, without a sled, traveling light. In fact, the only thing he carried was his lunch. He was surprised as he walked in the extreme cold. He had mittens on his hands and rubbed his nose and cheekbones, which felt numb from the cold. He had a full red beard, but the hair on his face did not protect his cheekbones or nose, which were still exposed to the frosty air.

A dog trotted at the man's heels—a big husky with a gray coat, very similar in temperament to his relative, the wild wolf. The dog was depressed by the freezing cold. He knew it was way too cold to be traveling. The dog's animal instincts were truer than the man's judgment. In reality, it was not just colder than fifty below zero—it was not just colder than sixty below—it was even colder than seventy below.

The dog certainly didn't know anything about thermometers. It couldn't think or reason like a man. But animal instinct told it everything it needed to know. The dog questioned every movement of the man, expecting him to find shelter and build a fire. The dog had learned about fire. The dog wanted the warmth of a fire, to burrow under the snow and cuddle up to keep warm away from the cold air.

Because of the extreme cold, the moisture from the dog's breathing settled on his fur, his face, even his eyelashes, as a fine frosty powder. The man's beard and moustache were covered with frost, just like the dog. It was so very cold that a muzzle of ice held his lips rigidly frozen.

The man walked on and stopped at a small stream. This was Henderson Creek. He knew he was only ten miles from a fork in the stream. He looked at his watch. It was ten o'clock. He was traveling at four miles an hour. He figured out that he would arrive at the fork at half-past twelve. He decided to celebrate that event by eating his lunch there.

The dog walked slowly at his heels with its tail drooping with discouragement as the man walked along the creek bed. The old sled trail was visible, but a dozen inches of snow covered the marks of the last sled that had traveled there. No one had come up or down this creek in more than a month. The man moved steadily on. There was no one to talk to; and had there been, speech would have been impossible because of the muzzle of ice on his mouth.

Once in a while he realized that it felt very cold. He had never experienced such cold. As he walked along, he rubbed his cheekbones and nose with the back of his mittened hands. But as much as he would rub, the instant he stopped, his cheekbones went numb; and an instant later, the end of his nose went numb. And frost covered his cheeks. He was sorry he hadn't devised a strap that would pass across his cheeks and save them from the biting cold. But then, it didn't matter much, after all. What were frosted cheeks? A bit painful, that was all; they were never serious.

The man always sharply noted where he placed his feet as he walked. Once, coming around a bend, he backed up abruptly like a startled horse and retreated several paces back along the trail. He knew the creek was frozen solid—clear to the bottom. No creek could contain water in this arctic winter. But he also knew that there were springs that bubbled out and ran along under the snow and on top of the ice of the creek. He knew that even the coldest snaps never froze these springs. And he knew their danger. They were traps. They hid pools of water under the snow that might be three inches deep, or three feet deep. Sometimes a layer of ice, half an inch thick, covered them, and that was in turn covered by the snow. Sometimes there were several layers of water and ice, so that when one took a step on what looked like snow, he would break through, getting himself wet to the waist in icy water.

That was why he had backed up in such a panic. He heard the crackle of the ice as it began to give way under his feet. To get his feet wet in such a cold temperature meant trouble and danger. At the very least, it meant delay, for he would be forced to stop and build a fire, and bare his feet while he dried his socks and moccasins. He stood and studied the creek and its banks and decided that the flow of the water came from the right. He thought for awhile, rubbing his nose and cheeks, then stepped gingerly to the left, testing the footing for each step. He made it safely through, took a fresh chew of tobacco, and continued along at his four-mile-an-hour gait.

In the course of the next two hours, he came upon several similar traps. Usually the snow above the hidden pools of water had a sunken, textured appearance that advertised the danger. Once again, however, he had a close call. And once, suspecting danger, he compelled the dog to walk out in front. The dog did not want to go. It hung back until the man shoved it forward. It then went quickly across the white unbroken surface.

Suddenly, it broke through. It floundered to one side and got away to firmer footing. It had wet its forefeet and legs. Almost immediately the water turned to ice. It made quick efforts to lick the ice off its legs. Then it dropped down in the snow and began to bite out the ice that formed between its toes. This was all a matter of instinct. To permit the ice to remain would mean sore feet. It did not know this. It did not think or reason. It merely obeyed the mysterious prompting that arose from the depth of its being. It acted on instinct. But the man knew, making a judgment on this situation, what needed to be done. He removed the mitten from his right hand and helped the dog tear out the ice particles. He did not expose his fingers for more than a minute and yet was astonished how swiftly they became numb. It was certainly cold. He pulled the mitten back on hastily and savagely beat his hand across his chest.

At twelve o'clock the day was at its brightest. Yet the sun still did not clear the horizon. The man walked under the clear, sunless sky and cast no shadow. At half past twelve to the minute, he arrived at the fork in the creek. He was pleased at the time he had made. If he kept up this pace, he would certainly be with his friends by six. He unbuttoned his jacket and took out his lunch. This action took no more than a few seconds, yet in that brief moment, his exposed fingers became numb. He did not put the mitten back on, but instead sharply struck his fingers against his leg to fight that numbness. Then he sat down on a snow-covered log to eat. The sensation he felt following striking his fingers against his leg disappeared so quickly that he was startled. He didn't even have a chance to take a bite of his biscuit. He struck his fingers repeatedly in a struggle against the numbness and returned them to his mitten, baring the other hand for the purpose of eating. He tried to take a mouthful, but the ice around his mouth prevented him from eating. He had forgotten to build a fire and thaw out. He chuckled at his foolishness. As he chuckled, he noticed the numbness creeping back into his exposed fingers. He also noted that the stinging which he had felt in his toes when he sat down was already passing away. He wondered whether his toes were warm or numb. He moved them inside his moccasins and decided they were numb.

He pulled his mitten on hurriedly and stood up. He was a bit frightened. He stamped up and down until the stinging returned to his feet. It was certainly cold. That old-timer he met from Sulphur Creek had spoken the truth when warning him how cold it sometimes got in the country. And he had laughed at him at the time. This showed him that one must not be too sure of things. There was no mistake about it. It was cold. He walked up and down, stamping his feet and thrashing his arms until he was reassured by the returning warmth. Then he got out matches and proceeded to make a fire. He dug down and found some seasoned twigs and branches lodged in the ground from the previous spring. Working carefully from a small beginning, he soon had a roaring fire over which he thawed the ice from his face. In the protection of the fire he ate his biscuits. For the moment, he had outwitted the cold. The dog too, took satisfaction in the fire, stretching out close enough for warmth and far enough away to escape being singed.

When the man finished eating, he filled his pipe and took his time having a smoke. Then he pulled on his mittens, settled the ear flaps of his cap firmly over his ears, and continued walking on the trail by the creek. The dog was disappointed and yearned to go back to the fire. The dog knew that it was not good to walk in such fearful cold. It was the time to lie snug in a hole in the snow and wait for the cold to be gone. But there was no intimacy between the dog and the man. The one was the slave of the other. The dog made no effort to communicate his apprehension to the man. It was not concerned about the welfare of the man. It was for its own sake that it yearned to return to the fire. But the man whistled and spoke to it with the threat of a whip. The dog swung in and followed at the man's heels.

For half an hour, the man saw no signs of danger of springs under the snow. And then it happened. At a place where there were no signs, where the soft unbroken snow seemed solid beneath, the ground broke through. It was not deep. He got wet halfway to the knees before he floundered out to firm ground.

He was angry. He cursed his luck aloud This would delay him an hour. He would have to build a fire and dry out his footgear. This was crucial at this low temperature—he knew that much.

He searched in the underbrush among the trunks of the small spruce trees and found a deposit of dry firewood—mostly sticks and twigs, but also larger pieces of seasoned branches and fine dry grasses from last year. He threw down several large pieces on top of the snow. This served as a foundation and prevented the young flame from being drowned in the melting snow. He got the flame started by touching a match to a small shred of birch bark that he took from his pocket. Placing it on the foundation, he fed the flame with wisps of dry grass and the tiniest dry twigs.

He worked slowly and carefully, keenly aware of danger. Gradually, as the flame grew stronger, he increased the size of the twigs. He squatted in the snow, pulling the twigs out and feeding them directly to the flame. He knew he must not fail. In such extreme cold, a man must not fail in his first attempt to build a fire—especially if his feet are wet. If his feet are dry, he can run along the trail and restore his circulation. But his feet were wet and freezing. No matter how fast he ran, his feet would only freeze harder.

Already all sensation was gone from his feet. To build the fire, he had been forced to remove his mittens, and his fingers had quickly gone numb. His pace of four miles per hour had kept his heart pumping blood to the surface of his body—to his extremities—his hands, his feet.

The blood had a life of its own, like the

dog. And like the dog, it wanted to hide away and cover itself up from the fearful cold. So long as he walked his four-miles-per-hour pace, he pumped blood to the surface. But now, it ebbed away and sank down into the recesses of his body. His extremities were the first to feel its absence. His wet feet froze faster. His exposed fingers numbed faster, though they had not yet begun to freeze. His nose and cheeks were already freezing, while the skin of all his body chilled as the blood failed to pump.

But he was safe. Toes and nose and cheeks would only be touched by the frost because the fire was beginning to burn with strength. He was feeding it twigs the size of his finger. In another minute he would be able to feed it with branches the size of his wrist. And then he could remove his wet footgear. While it dried he could keep his naked feet warm by the fire. The fire was a success. He was safe. He again remembered the advice of the old-timer and smiled. The old-timer had been very serious in laying down the law—no man should travel alone in the Yukon when it was fifty degrees below. Well, here he was. He had the accident. He was alone. And yet he had saved himself. Some of those old-timers were womanish, he thought. All a man had to do was keep his head, and he was all right. Any man who was a man could travel alone. But still, it was surprising how quickly his cheeks and nose were freezing. And he had not thought that his fingers could feel so lifeless in so short a time. But lifeless they were. He could scarcely make them move together to grip the twigs. And they seemed remote from his body and from him. When he touched a twig, he had to look to see whether he had hold of it. He was so numb that there was no sensation between him and his fingertips.

All of which meant little to him. There was the fire, snapping and crackling and promising life with each dancing flame. He started to untie his moccasins. They were coated with ice. His thick German socks were hard as sheets of iron going halfway to his knees. And the moccasin strings were like rods of steel, all twisted and knotted. For a moment he tugged at them with his numb fingers; then, realizing the folly of this, he drew his knife.

But before he could cut the strings, it happened. It was his own fault, or rather, mistake. He should not have built the fire under the spruce tree. He should have built it out in the open. But it had been easier to pull the twigs from the brush and drop them directly on the fire. Now, the tree under which he had done this carried a weight of snow on its branches. No wind had blown for weeks, so the snow had accumulated layer after layer, freezing on the branches. Each time he pulled a twig, it had shaken the tree. The movement was slight, as far as he was concerned, but enough to bring about the disaster. High up in the tree, one branch collapsed under the load of snow. This fell on the branches below, collapsing them. This process continued, spreading out and involving the whole tree. It grew like an avalanche and descended upon the man and the fire. The fire was blotted out! Where it had burned was a pile of fresh and disordered snow.

The man was shocked. It was as though he had just heard his sentence of death. For a moment he stopped and stared at the spot where the fire had been. Then he grew very calm. Perhaps that old-timer was right. If he had only had a trail mate, he would not be in danger now. The trail mate could have built the fire. Well, it was up to him alone to build the fire again. And the second time there must be no failure. Even if he succeeded, he would most likely lose some toes. His feet were badly frozen now, and it would be some time before the second fire was ready.

Such were his thoughts. But he did not sit and think them. He was busy all the time they were passing through his mind. He made a new foundation for a fire, this time out in the open where no treacherous tree could blot it out. Next he gathered dry grasses and tiny twigs. He could not bring his fingers together to grasp them, but he was able to gather them by the handful. In this way, however, he got many rotten twigs and bits of green moss that were undesirable, but it was the best he could do. He worked methodically, even collecting an armful of larger branches to be used later when the fire gathered strength. And all the while the dog sat and watched him, a certain wistfulness in its eyes, for it looked upon the man as the fire provider, and the fire was slow in coming.

When all was ready, the man reached in his pocket for a second piece of birch bark. He knew the bark was there, and though he could not feel it with his fingers, he could hear its crisp rustling as he fumbled for it. Try as he would, he could not clutch hold of it. And all the time he was aware that with each instant his feet were freezing. This thought tended to put him in a panic, but he fought against it and kept calm. He pulled on his mittens with his teeth, and swung his arms back and forth, beating his hands against his side with all his might. He did this sitting down, and he did it standing up. All the while the dog sat in the snow, its wolf brush of a tail curled warmly around its forefeet. Its sharp wolf ears pricked forward as it intently watched the man. And the man, as he beat and swung his arms and hands, felt a great surge of envy as he watched the creature that was warm and secure in its natural covering.

After a time he became aware of the first faraway signals of sensations in his fingers. The faint tingling grew stronger till it evolved into a stinging ache that was excruciating. But this gave the man satisfaction. He stripped the mitten from his right hand and grabbed the birch bark. His exposed fingers were quickly going numb again. Next he brought out his bunch of sulphur matches. But the tremendous cold had already driven the life out of his fingers. In his effort to separate one match from the others, the whole bunch fell into the snow. He tried to pick one out of the snow, but failed. His deadened fingers could neither clutch nor touch. He drove the thought of his freezing feet, and nose, and cheeks, out of his mind, devoting his whole soul to the matches. He watched, relying on his sense of vision in place of that of touch. When he saw his fingers on each side of the bunch, he closed them—that is, he willed them to close, but the fingers did not obey. He pulled the mitten on the right hand, and beat it fiercely against his knee. Then, with both mittened hands, he scooped the bunch of matches, along with much snow, into his lap. Yet he was no better off.

After some manipulation he managed to get the bunch between the heels of his mittened hands. Clutching them this way, he lifted them to his mouth. The ice crackled and snapped when, with a violent effort, he opened his mouth. He drew his lower jaw in, curled his upper lip out of the way, and scraped the bunch with his upper teeth to separate a match. He succeeded in getting one, which he dropped on his lap. He was no better off. He could not pick it up. Then he devised a way. He picked it up in his teeth and scratched it on his leg. He scratched it twenty times before he succeeded in lighting it. As it flamed, he held it to the birch bark with his teeth. But the smoke from the flames went up his nostrils and into his lungs, causing him to cough. The match fell into the snow and went out.

The old-timer had been right, he thought in this moment of controlled despair. After fifty below, a man should travel with a partner. He beat his hands, but failed in exciting any sensation. Suddenly he bared both hands, removing the mittens with his teeth. He caught the whole bunch between the heels of his hands. His arm muscles were not frozen, so he was able to press his hands tightly against the matches. Then he scratched the bunch along his leg. It flared into a flame, seventy sulphur matches at once! There was no wind to blow them out. He moved his head to one side to escape the suffocating fumes and held the blazing bunch to the birch bark. As he held it, he became aware of sensation in his hand. His flesh was burning. He could smell it. Deep down below the surface, he could feel it. The sensation developed into pain that became acute. And still he endured it, holding the flame of the matches clumsily to the bark. It would not light readily because his own burning hands were in the way, absorbing most of the flame.

At last, when he could endure no more, he jerked his hands apart. The blazing matches fell sizzling into the snow, but the birch bark was alight. He began laying dry grasses and the tiniest twigs on the flame. He could not pick and choose, for he had to use what he could lift between the heels of his hands. Small pieces of rotten wood and green moss clung to the twigs, and he bit them off as well as he could with his teeth. He cherished the flame, carefully and awkwardly. It meant life, and it must not perish. The lack of blood reaching the surface of his body now made him begin to shiver, and he grew more awkward. A large piece of green moss fell squarely on the little fire. He tried to poke it out with his fingers, but he couldn't control his shivering, and he disrupted the core of the little fire, causing the burning grasses and tiny twigs to separate and scatter. He tried to poke them together again, but despite the intensity of his effort, his shivering got in the way, and the twigs were hopelessly scattered. Each twig gushed a puff of smoke and went out. The fire provider had failed. As he looked around him, his eyes chanced upon the dog, sitting across the ruins of the fire in the snow. It was making restless, hunching movements, slightly lifting one foot and then the other, shifting its weight back and forth with wistful eagerness.

The sight of the dog put a wild idea into the man's head. He remembered the tale of a man, caught in a blizzard, who killed a steer and crawled inside the carcass and was saved. He would kill the dog and bury his hands in the warm body until the numbness went out of them. Then he could build another fire. He spoke to the dog, calling it to him. But in his voice was a strange note of fear that frightened the animal, who had never known the man to speak in such a way before. Something was the matter, and its suspicious nature sensed danger. It did not know what danger, but somewhere, somehow, in its brain arose an apprehension of the man. It flattened its ears down at the sound of the man's voice. Its restless, hunching movements and the shifting of its feet became more pronounced. But it would not come to the man. He got on his hands and knees and crawled toward the dog. This unusual posture again caused suspicion, and the animal sidled nervously away.

The man sat up in the snow for a moment and struggled for calmness. Then he pulled on his mittens, using his teeth, and got up on his feet. He glanced down at first to assure himself that he was really standing up. The absence of sensation in his feet left him unable to feel the earth beneath him. His erect position in itself started to drive the suspicion from the dog's mind, and when he spoke with a familiar sound, the dog responded with allegiance and came to him. As it came within reaching distance, the man lost his control. His arms flashed out to the dog, and he experienced genuine surprise when he discovered that his hands could not clutch. There was neither bend nor feeling in his fingers. He had forgotten for the moment that they were frozen and they were freezing more and more. All this happened quickly, and before the animal could get away, he encircled its body with his arms. He sat down in the snow, and he held the dog while it snarled, whined, and struggled.

But it was all he could do to hold its body encircled in his arms and sit there. He realized he could not kill the dog. There was no way to do it. With his helpless hands, he could neither draw nor hold his knife nor strangle the animal. He released it and it plunged wildly away, its tail between its legs, still snarling. It halted forty feet away and surveyed him curiously, with ears sharply pricked forward.

The man looked down at his hands in order to locate them and found them hanging at the ends of his arms. It struck him as curious that he should have to use his eyes in order to find out where his hands were. He began thrashing his arms back and forth, beating his mittened hands against his sides. He did this for five minutes, violently, and his heart pumped enough blood to the surface to put a stop to his shivering. But no sensation was aroused in his hands. He had the impression that they hung like weights on the ends of his arms. But he could not feel them.

A certain fear of death, dull and oppressive, came to him. This fear quickly became stronger as he realized that it was no longer a mere matter of freezing his fingers and toes, or of losing his hands of feet. This was a matter of life and death with the odds against him. This threw him into a panic, and he turned and ran along the old, dim trail. The dog joined in behind him and kept up with him. He ran blindly, without thought or intention, in fear such as he had never known in his life. Slowly, as he plowed and floundered through the snow, he began to see things again—the banks of the creek, the leafless trees, and the sky. The running made him feel better. He did not shiver. Maybe, if he ran on, his feet would thaw out; and anyway, if he ran far enough, he would reach camp and his friends. Without a doubt he would lose some fingers and toes and some of his face, but his friends would take care of him and save him when he got there. At the same time there was another thought in his mind that told him he would never get to the camp and his friends—that he would soon be stiff and dead. This thought he pushed into the background and refused to consider. Sometimes it pushed itself forward and demanded to be heard, but he thrust it back and tried to think of other things.

It struck him as curious that he could run at all on feet so frozen that he could not feel them as they struck the earth. It seemed as if he was skimming along above the surface, having no connection with the earth. His theory of running until he reached camp and his friends had one flaw in it; he lacked endurance. Several times he stumbled, and finally he crumpled up and fell. When he tried to rise, he failed. He must sit and rest, he decided, and next time he would merely walk and keep on going. As he sat and regained his breath, he noted that he was feeling quite warm and comfortable. He was not shivering, and it even seemed that a warm glow had come to his chest. And yet, when he touched his nose or cheeks, there was no sensation. Running would not thaw them out. Nor would it thaw out his hands and feet. Then the thought came to him that other parts of his body must now be freezing. He tried to keep this thought down, to forget it, to think of something else. He was aware of the panicky feeling that it caused, and he was afraid to panic. But the thought persisted until it produced a vision in his mind of his body totally frozen. This was too much, and he made another wild run along the trail. He slowed down to a walk, but the thought of the freezing extending through his body made him run again.

And all the time the dog ran with him at his heels. When he fell down a second time, it curled its tail over its forefeet and sat in front of him, facing him, curiously eager and intent. The warmth and security of the animal angered him, and he cursed it till it flattened down its ears. This time the shivering came more quickly upon the man. He was losing his battle with the frost. It was creeping into his body from all sides. The thought of it drove him on, but he ran no more than a hundred feet when he staggered and pitched headlong into the ground. It was his last panic. When he recovered his breath and control, he sat up and in his mind, entertained the concept of meeting death with dignity. His idea of it was that he had been making a fool of himself, running around like a chicken with its head cut off—such was the image that occurred to him. Well, he was bound to freeze anyway, and he might as well take it decently. With this newfound peace of mind came the first glimmers of drowsiness. A good idea, he thought, to sleep off to death. It was like taking an anesthetic. Freezing was not as bad as people thought. There were a lot of worse ways to die.

He pictured his friends finding his body the next day. Suddenly, he imagined himself with them, coming along the trail and looking for himself. And still with them, he came around a turn in the trail and found himself lying in the snow. He did not belong with himself anymore, for even then he was out of himself, standing with his friends and looking at himself in the snow. *It certainly was cold* was his thought. When he got back to the States, he could tell his folks what *real* cold was. He drifted on from this vision to the old-timer on Sulphur Creek. He could see him quite clearly, warm and comfortable, smoking a pipe.

"You were right, old-timer; you were right," the man mumbled.

Then he dozed off into what seemed to him the most comfortable and satisfying sleep he had ever known. The dog sat facing him and waiting. The brief day drew to a close in a long, slow twilight. There were no signs of a fire to be made. Never in the dog's experience had it known a man to sit like that in the snow and make no fire. As the twilight drew on, the dog's yearning for the fire took over. It whined softly and then flattened its ears down in anticipation of being scolded by the man. But the man remained silent. Later the dog whined loudly. And still later, it crept close to the man and caught the scent of death. This made the animal bristle and back away. It waited a little longer, howling under the stars that danced and shone brightly in the cold sky. Then it turned and trotted up the trail in the direction of the camp it knew, where there were other food providers and fire providers. ■

PREVIEW

Hunting—big-game hunting—has been Sanger Rainsford's life. When an accident at sea strands him on an island, he is lucky enough to be rescued by General Zaroff, who is not only charming and helpful, but who shares Rainsford's passion. But relief soon turns to horror when Rainsford learns the secret of Zaroff's "most dangerous game."

THE MOST DANGEROUS GAME

Richard Connell

"Off there to the right—somewhere—is a large island," said Whitney. "It's rather a mystery—"

"What island is it?" Rainsford asked.

"The old charts call it 'Ship-Trap Island,'" Whitney replied. "A suggestive name, isn't it? Sailors have a curious dread of the place. I don't know why. Some superstition—"

"Can't see it," remarked Rainsford, trying to peer through the dank tropical night that was palpable as it pressed its thick warm blackness in upon the yacht.

"You've good eyes," said Whitney, with a laugh, "and I've seen you pick off a moose moving in the brown fall bush at four hundred yards, but even you can't see four miles or so through a moonless Caribbean night."

"Nor four yards," admitted Rainsford. "Ugh! It's like moist black velvet."

"It will be light enough in Rio," promised Whitney. "We should make it in a few days. I hope the jaguar guns have come from Purdey's.[1] We should have some good hunting up the Amazon. Great sport, hunting."

"The best sport in the world," agreed Rainsford.

"For the hunter," amended Whitney. "Not for the jaguar."

"Don't talk rot, Whitney," said Rainsford. "You're a big-game hunter, not a philosopher. Who cares how a jaguar feels?"

"Perhaps the jaguar does," observed Whitney.

"Bah! They've no understanding."

"Even so, I rather think they understand one thing—fear. The fear of pain and the fear of death."

"Nonsense," laughed Rainsford. "This hot weather is making you soft, Whitney. Be a realist. The world is made up of two classes—the hunters and the huntees. Luckily, you and I are hunters. Do you think we've passed that island yet?"

"I can't tell in the dark. I hope so."

"Why?" asked Rainsford.

"The place has a reputation—a bad one."

"Cannibals?" suggested Rainsford.

"Hardly. Even cannibals wouldn't live in such a God-forsaken place. But it's gotten into sailor lore, somehow. Didn't you notice that the crew's nerves seemed a bit jumpy today?"

"They were a bit strange, now you mention it. Even Captain Nielsen—"

"Yes, even that tough-minded old Swede, who'd go up to the devil himself and ask him for a light. Those fishy blue eyes held a look I never saw there before. All I could get out of him was 'This place has an evil name among seafaring men, sir.' Then he said to me, very gravely, 'Don't you feel anything?'—as if the air about us was actually poisonous. Now, you mustn't laugh when I tell you this—I did feel something like a sudden chill.

"There was no breeze. The sea was as flat as a plate-glass window. We were drawing near the island then. What I felt was a—a mental chill; a sort of sudden dread."

"Pure imagination," said Rainsford.

"One superstitious sailor can taint the whole ship's company with his fear."

"Maybe. But sometimes I think sailors have an extra sense that tells them when they are in danger. Sometimes I think evil is a tangible thing—with wavelengths, just as sound and light have. An evil place can, so to speak, broadcast vibrations of evil. Anyhow, I'm glad we're getting out of this zone. Well, I think I'll turn in now, Rainsford."

"I'm not sleepy," said Rainsford. "I'm going to smoke another pipe up on the after-deck."

"Good night, then, Rainsford. See you at breakfast."

"Right. Good night, Whitney."

There was no sound in the night as Rainsford sat there but the muffled throb of the engine that drove the yacht swiftly through the darkness, and the swish and ripple of the wash of the propeller.

Rainsford, reclining in a steamer chair, indolently puffed on his favorite brier. The sensuous drowsiness of the night was on him. "It's so dark," he thought, "that I could sleep without closing my eyes; the night would be my eyelids—"

An abrupt sound startled him. Off to the right he heard it, and his ears, expert in such matters, could not be mistaken. Again he heard the sound, and again. Somewhere, off in the blackness, someone had fired a gun three times.

Rainsford sprang up and moved quickly to the rail, mystified. He strained his eyes in the direction from which the reports had come, but it was like trying to see through a blanket. He leaped upon the rail and balanced himself there, to get greater elevation; his pipe, striking a rope, was knocked from his mouth. He lunged for it; a short, hoarse cry came from his lips as he realized he had reached too far and had lost his balance. The cry was pinched off short as the blood-warm waters of the Caribbean Sea closed over his head.

He struggled up to the surface and tried to cry out, but the wash from the speeding yacht slapped him in the face and the salt water in his open mouth made him gag and strangle. Desperately he struck out with strong strokes after the receding lights of the yacht, but he stopped before he had swum fifty feet. A certain coolheadedness had come to him; it was not the first time he had been in a tight place. There was a chance that his cries could be heard by someone aboard the yacht, but that chance was slender and grew more slender as the yacht raced on. He wrestled himself out of his clothes and shouted with all his power. The lights of the yacht became faint and ever-vanishing fireflies; then they were blotted out entirely by the night.

Rainsford remembered the shots. They had come from the right, and doggedly he swam in that direction, swimming with slow, deliberate strokes, conserving his strength. For a seemingly endless time he fought the sea. He began to count his strokes; he could do possibly a hundred more and then—

Rainsford heard a sound. It came out of the darkness, a high screaming sound, the sound of an animal in an extremity of anguish and terror.

He did not recognize the animal that made the sound; he did not try to; with fresh vitality he swam toward the sound. He heard it again; then it was cut short by another noise, crisp, staccato.

"Pistol shot," muttered Rainsford, swimming on.

Ten minutes of determined effort brought another sound to his ears—the most welcome he had ever heard—the muttering and growling of the sea breaking on a rocky shore. He was almost on the rocks before he saw them; on a night less calm he would have been shattered against them. With his remaining strength he dragged himself from the swirling waters. Jagged crags appeared to jut up into the opaqueness; he forced himself upward, hand over hand. Gasping, his hands raw, he reached a flat place at the top. Dense jungle came down to the very edge of the cliffs. What perils that tangle of trees and underbrush might hold for him did not concern Rainsford just then. All he knew was that he was safe from his enemy, the sea, and that utter weariness was on him. He flung himself down at the jungle edge and tumbled headlong into the deepest sleep of his life.

When he opened his eyes, he knew from the position of the sun that it was late in the afternoon. Sleep had given him new vigor; a sharp hunger was picking at him. He looked about him, almost cheerfully.

"Where there are pistol shots, there are men. Where there are men, there is food," he thought. But what kind of men, he wondered, in so forbidding a place? An unbroken front of snarled and ragged jungle fringed the shore.

He saw no sign of a trail through the closely knit web of weeds and trees; it was easier to go along the shore, and Rainsford floundered along by the water. Not far from where he landed, he stopped.

Some wounded thing—by the evidence, a large animal—had thrashed about in the underbrush; the jungle weeds were crushed down and the moss was lacerated; one patch of weeds was stained crimson. A small, glittering object not far away caught Rainsford's eye and he picked it up. It was an empty cartridge.

"A twenty-two," he remarked. "That's odd. It must have been a fairly large animal too. The hunter had his nerve with him to tackle it with a light gun. It's clear that the brute put up a fight. I suppose the first three shots I heard was when the hunter flushed his quarry and wounded it. The last shot was when he trailed it here and finished it."

He examined the ground closely and found what he had hoped to find—the print of hunting boots. They pointed along the cliff in the direction he had been going. Eagerly he hurried along, now slipping on a rotten log or a loose stone, but making headway; night was beginning to settle down on the island.

Bleak darkness was blacking out the sea and jungle when Rainsford sighted the lights. He came upon them as he turned a crook in the coast line; and his first thought was that he had come upon a village, for there were many lights. But as he forged along he saw to his great astonishment that all the lights were in one enormous building—a lofty structure with pointed towers plunging upward into the gloom. His eyes made out the shadowy outlines of a palatial chateau; it was set on a high bluff, and on three sides of it cliffs dived down to where the sea licked greedy lips in the shadows.

"Mirage," thought Rainsford. But it was no mirage, he found, when he opened the tall spiked iron gate. The stone steps were real enough; the massive door with a leering gargoyle for a knocker was real enough; yet above it all hung an air of unreality.

He lifted the knocker, and it creaked up stiffly, as if it had never before been used. He let it fall, and it startled him with its booming loudness. He thought he heard steps within; the door remained closed. Again Rainsford lifted the heavy knocker and let it fall. The door opened then—opened as suddenly as if it were on a spring—and Rainsford stood blinking in the river of glaring gold light that poured out. The first thing Rainsford's eyes discerned was the largest man Rainsford had ever seen—a gigantic creature, solidly made and black-bearded to the waist. In his hand the man held a long-barreled revolver, and he was pointing it straight at Rainsford's heart.

Out of the snarl of beard two small eyes regarded Rainsford.

"Don't be alarmed," said Rainsford, with a smile which he hoped was disarming. "I'm no robber. I fell off a yacht. My name is Sanger Rainsford of New York City."

The menacing look in the eyes did not change. The revolver pointing as rigidly as if the giant were a statue. He gave no sign that he understood Rainsford's words, or that he had even heard them. He was dressed in uniform—a black uniform trimmed with gray astrakhan.[2]

"I'm Sanger Rainsford of New York," Rainsford began again. "I fell off a yacht. I am hungry."

The man's only answer was to raise with his thumb the hammer of his revolver. Then Rainsford saw the man's free hand go to his forehead in a military salute, and he saw him click his heels together and stand at attention. Another man was coming down the broad marble steps, an erect, slender man in evening clothes. He advanced to Rainsford and held out his hand.

In a cultivated voice marked by a slight accent that gave it added precision and deliberateness, he said, "It is a very great pleasure and honor to welcome Mr. Sanger Rainsford, the celebrated hunter, to my home."

Automatically Rainsford shook the man's hand.

"I've read your book about hunting snow leopards in Tibet, you see," explained the man. "I am General Zaroff."

Rainsford's first impression was that the man was singularly handsome; his second was that there was an original, almost bizarre quality about the general's face. He was a tall man past middle age, for his hair was a vivid white; but his thick eyebrows and pointed military mustache were as black as the night from which Rainsford had come. His eyes, too, were black and very bright. He had high cheekbones, a sharpcut nose, a spare, dark face—the face of a man used to giving orders, the face of an aristocrat. Turning to the giant in uniform, the general made a sign. The giant put away his pistol, saluted, withdrew.

"Ivan is an incredibly strong fellow," remarked the general, "but he has the misfortune to be deaf and dumb. A simple fellow, but, I'm afraid, like all his race, a bit of a savage."

"Is he Russian?"

"He is a Cossack," said the general, and

his smile showed red lips and pointed teeth. "So am I."

"Come," he said, "we shouldn't be chatting here. We can talk later. Now you want clothes, food, rest. You shall have them. This is a most restful spot."

Ivan had reappeared, and the general spoke to him with lips that moved but gave forth no sound.

"Follow Ivan, if you please, Mr. Rainsford," said the general. "I was about to have my dinner when you came. I'll wait for you. You'll find that my clothes will fit you, I think."

It was to a huge, beam-ceilinged bedroom with a canopied bed big enough for six men that Rainsford followed the silent giant. Ivan laid out an evening suit, and Rainsford, as he put it on, noticed that it came from a London tailor who ordinarily cut and sewed for none below the rank of duke.

The dining room to which Ivan conducted him was in many ways remarkable. There was a medieval magnificence about it; it suggested a baronial hall of feudal times with its oaken panels, its high ceiling, its vast refectory tables where twoscore men could sit down to eat. About the hall were mounted heads of many animals—lions, tigers, elephants, moose, bears; larger or more perfect specimens Rainsford had never seen. At the great table the general was sitting, alone.

"You'll have a cocktail, Mr. Rainsford," he suggested. The cocktail was surpassingly good; and, Rainsford noted, the table appointments were of the finest—the linen, the crystal, the silver, the china.

They were eating *borsch*, the rich, red soup with whipped cream so dear to Russian palates. Half apologetically General Zaroff said, "We do our best to preserve the amenities of civilization here. Please forgive any lapses. We are well off the beaten track, you know. Do you think the champagne has suffered from its long ocean trip?"

"Not in the least," declared Rainsford. He was finding the general a most thoughtful and affable host, a true cosmopolite. But there was one small trait of the general's that made Rainsford uncomfortable. Whenever he looked up from his plate he found the general studying him, appraising him narrowly.

"Perhaps," said General Zaroff, "you were surprised that I recognized your name. You see, I read all books on hunting published in English, French, and Russian. I have but one passion in my life, Mr. Rainsford, and it is the hunt."

"You have some wonderful heads here," said Rainsford as he ate a particularly well-cooked filet mignon. "That Cape buffalo is the largest I ever saw."

"Oh, that fellow. Yes, he was a monster."

"Did he charge you?"

"Hurled me against a tree," said the general. "Fractured my skull. But I got the brute."

"I've always thought," said Rainsford, "that the Cape buffalo is the most dangerous of all big game."

For a moment the general did not reply; he was smiling his curious red-lipped smile. Then he said slowly, "No. You are wrong, sir. The Cape buffalo is not the most dangerous big game." He sipped his wine. "Here in my preserve on this island," he said in the same slow tone, "I hunt more dangerous game."

Rainsford expressed his surprise. "Is there big game on this island?"

The general nodded. "The biggest."

"Really?"

"Oh, it isn't here naturally, of course. I have to stock the island."

"What have you imported, general?" Rainsford asked. "Tigers?"

The general smiled. "No," he said.

"Hunting tigers ceased to interest me some years ago. I exhausted their possibilities, you see. No thrill left in tigers, no real danger. I live for danger, Mr. Rainsford."

The general took from his pocket a gold cigarette case and offered his guest a long black cigarette with a silver tip; it was perfumed and gave off a smell like incense.

"We will have some capital hunting, you and I," said the general. "I shall be most glad to have your society."

"But what game—" began Rainsford.

"I'll tell you," said the general. "You will be amused, I know. I think I may say, in all modesty, that I have done a rare thing. I have invented a new sensation. May I pour you another glass of port?"

"Thank you, general."

The general filled both glasses, and said, "God makes some men poets. Some He makes kings, some beggars. Me He made a hunter. My hand was made for the trigger, my father said. He was a very rich man with a quarter of a million acres in the Crimea, and he was an ardent sportsman. When I was only five years old, he gave me a little gun, specially made in Moscow for me, to shoot sparrows with. When I shot some of his prize turkeys with it, he did not punish me; he complimented me on my marksmanship. I killed my first bear in the Caucasus when I was ten. My whole life has been one prolonged hunt. I went into the army—it was expected of noblemen's sons—and for a time commanded a division of Cossack cavalry, but my real interest was always the hunt. I have hunted every kind of game in every land. It would be impossible for me to tell you how many animals I have killed."

The general puffed at his cigarette.

"After the debacle in Russia[3] I left the country, for it was imprudent for an officer of the Czar to stay there. Many noble Russians lost everything. I, luckily, had invested heavily in American securities, so I shall never have to open a tearoom in Monte Carlo or drive a taxi in Paris. Naturally, I continued to hunt—grizzlies in your Rockies, crocodiles in the Ganges, rhinoceroses in East Africa. It was in Africa that the Cape buffalo hit me and laid me up for six months. As soon as I recovered, I started for the Amazon to hunt jaguars, for I had heard they were unusually cunning. They weren't." The Cossack sighed. "They were no match at all for a hunter with his wits about him and a high-powered rifle. I was bitterly disappointed. I was lying in my tent with a splitting headache one night when a terrible thought pushed its way into my mind. Hunting was beginning to bore me! And hunting, remember, had been my life. I have heard that in America businessmen often go to pieces when they give up the business that has been their life."

"Yes, that's so," said Rainsford.

The general smiled. "I had no wish to go to pieces," he said. "I must do something. Now, mine is an analytical mind, Mr. Rainsford. Doubtless that is why I enjoy the problems of the chase."

"No doubt, General Zaroff."

"So," continued the general, "I asked myself why the hunt no longer fascinated me. You are much younger than I am, Mr. Rainsford, and have not hunted as much, but you perhaps can guess the answer."

"What was it?"

"Simply this: hunting had ceased to be what you call 'a sporting proposition.' It had become too easy. I always got my quarry. Always. There is no greater bore than perfection."

The general lit a fresh cigarette.

"No animal had a chance with me any more. That is no boast; it is a mathematical certainty. The animal had nothing but his legs and his instinct. Instinct is no match for reason. When I thought of this it was a tragic moment for me, I can tell you."

Rainsford leaned across the table, absorbed in what his host was saying.

"It came to me as an inspiration what I must do," the general went on.

"And that was?"

The general smiled the quiet smile of one who has faced an obstacle and surmounted it with success. "I had to invent a new animal to hunt," he said.

"A new animal? You're joking."

"Not at all," said the general. "I never joke about hunting. I needed a new animal. I found one. So I bought this island, built this house, and here I do my hunting. The island is perfect for my purposes—there are jungles with a maze of traits in them, hills, swamps—"

"But the animal, General Zaroff?"

"Oh," said the general, "it supplies me with the most exciting hunting in the world. No other hunting compares with it for an instant. Every day I hunt, and I never grow bored now, for I have a quarry with which I can match my wits."

Rainsford's bewilderment showed in his face.

"I wanted the ideal animal to hunt," explained the general. "So I said, 'What are the attributes of an ideal quarry?' And the answer was, of course, 'It must have courage, cunning, and, above all, it must be able to reason.'"

"But no animal can reason," objected Rainsford.

"My dear fellow," said the general, "there is one that can."

"But you can't mean—" gasped Rainsford.

"And why not?"

"I can't believe you are serious, General Zaroff. This is a grisly joke."

"Why should I not be serious? I am speaking of hunting."

"Hunting? Great Guns, General Zaroff, what you speak of is murder."

The general laughed with entire good nature. He regarded Rainsford quizzically. "I refuse to believe that so modern and civilized a young man as you seem to be harbors romantic ideas about the value of human life. Surely your experiences in the war—"

"Did not make me condone cold-blooded murder," finished Rainsford stiffly.

Laughter shook the general. "How extraordinarily droll you are!" he said. "One does not expect nowadays to find a young man of the educated class, even in America, with such a naive, and, if I may say so, mid-Victorian point of view. It's like finding a snuffbox in a limousine. Ah, well, doubtless you had Puritan ancestors. So many Americans appear to have had. I'll wager you'll forget your notions when you go hunting with me. You've a genuine new thrill in store for you, Mr. Rainsford."

"Thank you, I'm a hunter, not a murderer."

"Dear me," said the general, quite unruffled, "again that unpleasant word. But I think I can show you that your scruples are quite ill founded."

"Yes?"

"Life is for the strong, to be lived by the strong, and, if needs be, taken by the strong. The weak of the world were put here to give the strong pleasure. I am strong. Why should I not use my gift? If I wish to hunt, why should I not? I hunt the scum of the earth: sailors from tramp ships—lascars,[4] blacks, Chinese, whites, mongrels—a thoroughbred horse or hound is worth more than a score of them."

"But they are men," said Rainsford hotly.

"Precisely," said the general. "That is why I use them. It gives me pleasure. They can reason, after a fashion. So they are dangerous."

"But where do you get them?"

The general's left eyelid fluttered down in a wink. "This island is called Ship Trap," he answered. "Sometimes an angry god of the high seas sends them to me. Sometimes, when Providence is not so kind, I help Providence a bit. Come to the window with me."

Rainsford went to the window and looked out toward the sea.

"Watch! Out there!" exclaimed the general, pointing into the night. Rainsford's eyes saw only blackness, and then, as the general pressed a button, far out to sea Rainsford saw the flash of lights.

The general chuckled. "They indicate a channel," he said, "where there's none; giant rocks with razor edges crouch like a sea monster with wide-open jaws. They can crush a ship as easily as I crush this nut." He dropped a walnut on the hardwood floor and brought his heel grinding down on it. "Oh, yes," he said, casually, as if in answer to a question, "I have electricity. We try to be civilized here."

"Civilized? And you shoot down men?"

A trace of anger was in the general's black eyes, but it was there for but a second; and he said, in his most pleasant manner, "Dear me, what a righteous young man you are! I assure you I do not do the thing you suggest. That would be barbarous. I treat these visitors with every consideration. They get plenty of good food and exercise. They get into splendid physical condition. You shall see for yourself tomorrow."

"What do you mean?"

"We'll visit my training school," smiled the general. "It's in the cellar. I have about a dozen pupils down there now. They're from the Spanish bark *San Lucar* that had the bad luck to go on the rocks out there. A very inferior lot, I regret to say. Poor specimens and more accustomed to the deck than to the jungle." He raised his hand, and Ivan, who served as waiter, brought thick Turkish coffee. Rainsford, with an effort, held his tongue in check.

"It's a game, you see," pursued the general blandly. "I suggest to one of them that we go hunting. I give him a supply of food and an excellent hunting knife. I give him three hours' start. I am to follow, armed only with a pistol of the smallest caliber and range. If my quarry eludes me for three whole days, he wins the game. If I find him"—the general smiled—"he loses."

"Suppose he refuses to be hunted?"

"Oh," said the general, "I give him his option, of course. He need not play that game if he doesn't wish to. If he does not wish to hunt, I turn him over to Ivan. Ivan once had the honor of serving as official knouter[5] to the Great White Czar,[6] and he has his own ideas of sport. Invariably, Mr. Rainsford, invariably they choose the hunt."

"And if they win?"

The smile on the general's face widened. "To date I have not lost," he said. Then he added, hastily: "I don't wish you to think me a braggart, Mr. Rainsford. Many of them afford only the most elementary sort of problem. Occasionally I strike a tartar. One almost did win. I eventually had to use the dogs."

"The dogs?"

"This way, please. I'll show you."

The general steered Rainsford to a window. The lights from the windows sent a flickering illumination that made grotesque patterns on the courtyard below, and Rainsford could see moving about there a dozen or so huge black shapes; as they turned toward him, their eyes glittered greenly.

"A rather good lot, I think," observed the general. "They are let out at seven every night. If anyone should try to get into my house—or out of it—something extremely regrettable would occur to him." He hummed a snatch of song from the Folies Bergere.[7]

"And now," said the general, "I want to show you my new collection of heads. Will you come with me to the library?"

"I hope," said Rainsford, "that you will excuse me tonight, General Zaroff. I'm really not feeling well."

"Ah, indeed?" the general inquired solicitously. "Well, I suppose that's only natural, after your long swim. You need a good, restful night's sleep. Tomorrow you'll feel like a new man, I'll wager. Then we'll hunt, eh? I've one rather promising prospect—" Rainsford was hurrying from the room.

"Sorry you can't go with me tonight," called the general. "I expect rather fair sport—a big, strong, black. He looks resourceful—Well, good night, Mr. Rainsford; I hope you have a good night's rest."

The bed was good, and the pajamas of the softest silk, and he was tired in every fiber of his being, but nevertheless Rainsford could not quiet his brain with the opiate of sleep. He lay, eyes wide open. Once he thought he heard stealthy steps in the corridor outside his room. He sought to throw open the door; it would not open. He went to the window and looked out. His room was high up in one of the towers. The lights of the chateau were out now, and it was dark and silent; but there was a fragment of sallow moon, and by its wan light he could see, dimly, the courtyard. There, weaving in and out in the pattern of shadow, were black, noiseless forms; the hounds heard him at the window and looked up, expectantly, with their green eyes. Rainsford went back to the bed and lay down. By many methods he tried to put himself to sleep. He had achieved a doze when, just as morning began to come, he heard, far off in the jungle, the faint report of a pistol.

General Zaroff did not appear until luncheon. He was dressed faultlessly in the tweeds of a country squire. He was solicitous about the state of Rainsford's health.

"As for me," sighed the general, "I do not feel so well. I am worried, Mr. Rainsford. Last night I detected traces of my old complaint."

To Rainsford's questioning glance the general said, "Ennui. Boredom."

Then, taking a second helping of crêpes Suzette, the general explained: "The hunting was not good last night. The fellow lost his head. He made a straight trail that offered no problems at all. That's the trouble with these sailors; they have dull brains to begin with, and they do not know how to get about in the woods. They do excessively stupid and obvious things. It's most annoying. Will you have another glass of Chablis, Mr. Rainsford?"

"General," said Rainsford firmly, "I wish to leave this island at once."

The general raised his thickets of eyebrows; he seemed hurt. "But, my dear fellow," the general protested, "you've only just come. You've had no hunting—"

"I wish to go today," said Rainsford. He saw the dead black eyes of the general on him, studying him. General Zaroff's face suddenly brightened.

He filled Rainsford's glass with venerable Chablis from a dusty bottle.

"Tonight," said the general, "we will hunt—you and I."

Rainsford shook his head. "No, general," he said. "I will not hunt."

The general shrugged his shoulders and delicately ate a hothouse grape. "As you wish, my friend," he said. "The choice rests entirely with you. But may I not venture to suggest that you will find my idea of sport more diverting than Ivan's?"

He nodded toward the corner to where the giant stood, scowling, his thick arms crossed on his hogshead of chest.

"You don't mean—" cried Rainsford.

"My dear fellow," said the general, "have I not told you I always mean what I say about hunting? This is really an inspiration. I drink to a foeman worthy of my steel—at last." The general raised his glass, but Rainsford sat staring at him.

"You'll find this game worth playing," the general said enthusiastically. "Your brain against mine. Your woodcraft against mine. Your strength and stamina against mine. Outdoor chess! And the stake is not without value, eh?"

"And if I win—" began Rainsford huskily.

"I'll cheerfully acknowledge myself defeated if I do not find you by midnight of the third day," said General Zaroff. "My sloop will place you on the mainland near a town." The general read what Rainsford was thinking.

"Oh, you can trust me," said the Cossack. "I will give you my word as a gentleman and a sportsman. Of course you, in turn, must agree to say nothing of your visit here."

"I'll agree to nothing of the kind," said Rainsford.

"Oh," said the general, "in that case— But why discuss that now? Three days hence we can discuss it over a bottle of Veuve Cliquot, unless—"

The general sipped his wine.

Then a businesslike air animated him. "Ivan," he said to Rainsford, "will supply you with hunting clothes, food, a knife. I suggest you wear moccasins; they leave a poorer trail. I suggest, too, that you avoid the big swamp in the southeast corner of the island. We call it Death Swamp. There's quicksand there. One foolish fellow tried it. The deplorable part of it was that Lazarus followed him. You can imagine my feelings, Mr. Rainsford. I loved Lazarus; he was the finest hound in my pack. Well, I must beg you to excuse me now. I always take a siesta after lunch. You'll hardly have time for a nap, I fear. You'll want to start, no doubt. I shall not follow till dusk. Hunting at night is so much more exciting than by day, don't you think? Au revoir, Mr. Rainsford, au revoir." General Zaroff, with a deep, courtly bow, strolled from the room.

From another door came Ivan. Under one arm he carried khaki hunting clothes, a haversack of food, a leather sheath containing a long-bladed hunting knife; his right hand rested on a cocked revolver thrust in the crimson sash about his waist. . . .

Rainsford had fought his way through the bush for two hours. "I must keep my nerve. I must keep my nerve," he said through tight teeth.

He had not been entirely clear-headed when the chateau gates snapped shut behind him. His whole idea at first was to put distance between himself and General Zaroff; and, to this end, he had plunged along, spurred on by the sharp rowels of something very like panic. Now he had got a grip on himself, had stopped, and was taking stock of himself and the situation. He saw that straight flight was futile; inevitably it would bring him face to face with the sea. He was in a picture with a frame of water, and his operations, clearly, must take place within that frame.

"I'll give him a trail to follow," muttered Rainsford, and he struck off from the rude path he had been following into the trackless wilderness. He executed a series of intricate loops; he doubled on his trail again and again, recalling all the lore of the fox hunt, and all the dodges of the fox. Night found him leg-weary, with hands and face lashed by the branches, on a thickly wooded ridge. He knew it would be insane to blunder on through the dark, even if he had the strength. His need for rest was imperative, and he thought, "I have played the fox; now I must play the cat of the fable." A big tree with a thick trunk and outspread branches was near-by, and, taking care to leave not the slightest mark, he climbed up into the crotch, and, stretching out on one of the broad limbs, after a fashion, rested. Rest brought him new confidence and almost a feeling of security. Even so zealous a hunter as General Zaroff could not trace him there, he told himself; only the devil himself could follow that complicated trail through the jungle after dark. But perhaps the general was a devil—

An apprehensive night crawled slowly by like a wounded snake, and sleep did not visit Rainsford, although the silence of a dead world was on the jungle. Toward morning when a dingy gray was varnishing the sky, the cry of some startled bird focused Rainsford's attention in that direction. Something was coming through the bush, coming slowly, carefully, coming by the same winding way Rainsford had come. He flattened himself down on the limb, and through a screen of leaves almost as thick as tapestry, he watched. The thing that was approaching was a man.

It was General Zaroff. He made his way along with his eyes fixed in utmost concentration on the ground before him. He paused, almost beneath the tree, dropped to his knees and studied the ground. Rainsford's impulse was to hurl himself down like a panther, but he saw that the general's right hand held something metallic—a small automatic pistol.

The hunter shook his head several times, as if he were puzzled. Then he straightened up and took from his case one of his black cigarettes; its pungent incense-like smoke floated up to Rainsford's nostrils.

Rainsford held his breath. The general's eyes had left the ground and were traveling inch by inch up the tree. Rainsford froze there, every muscle tensed for a spring. But the sharp eyes of the hunter stopped before they reached the limb where Rainsford lay; a smile spread over his brown face. Very deliberately he blew a smoke ring into the air; then he turned his back on the tree and walked carelessly away, back along the trail he had come. The swish of the underbrush against his hunting boots grew fainter and fainter.

The pent-up air burst hotly from

Rainsford's lungs. His first thought made him feel sick and numb. The general could follow a trail through the woods at night; he could follow an extremely difficult trail; he must have uncanny powers; only by the merest chance had the Cossack failed to see his quarry.

Rainsford's second thought was even more terrible. It sent a shudder of cold horror through his whole being. Why had the general smiled? Why had he turned back?

Rainsford did not want to believe what his reason told him was true, but the truth was as evident as the sun that had by now pushed through the morning mists. The general was playing with him! The general was saving him for another day's sport! The Cossack was the cat; he was the mouse. Then it was that Rainsford knew the full meaning of terror.

"I will not lose my nerve. I will not."

He slid down from the tree and struck off again into the woods. His face was set, and he forced the machinery of his mind to function. Three hundred yards from his hiding place, he stopped where a huge dead tree leaned precariously on a smaller, living one. Throwing off his sack of food, Rainsford took his knife from its sheath and began to work with all his energy.

The job was finished at last, and he threw himself down behind a fallen log a hundred feet away. He did not have to wait long. The cat was coming again to play with the mouse.

Following the trail with the sureness of a bloodhound came General Zaroff. Nothing escaped those searching black eyes, no crushed blade of grass, no bent twig, no mark, no matter how faint, in the moss. So intent was the Cossack on his stalking that he was upon the thing Rainsford had made before he saw it. His foot touched the protruding bough that was the trigger. Even as he touched it, the general sensed his danger and leaped back with the agility of an ape. But he was not quite quick enough; the dead tree, delicately adjusted to rest on the cut living one, crashed down and struck the general a glancing blow on the shoulder as it fell; but for his alertness, he must have been smashed beneath it. He staggered, but he did not fall; nor did he drop his revolver. He stood there, rubbing his injured shoulder, and Rainsford, with fear again gripping his heart, heard the general's mocking laugh ring through the jungle.

"Rainsford," called the general, "if you are within sound of my voice, as I suppose you are, let me congratulate you. Not many men know how to make a Malay mancatcher. Luckily for me I, too, have hunted in Malacca. You are proving interesting, Mr. Rainsford. I am going now to have my wound dressed; it's only a slight one. But I shall be back. I shall be back."

When the general, nursing his bruised shoulder, had gone, Rainsford took up his flight again. It was flight now, a desperate, hopeless flight, that carried him on for some hours. Dusk came, then darkness, and still he pressed on. The ground grew softer under his moccasins; the vegetation grew ranker, denser; insects bit him savagely.

Then, as he stepped forward, his foot sank into the ooze. He tried to wrench it back, but the muck sucked viciously at his foot as if it were a giant leech. With a violent effort, he tore his feet loose. He knew where he was now. Death Swamp and its quicksand.

His hands were tight closed as if his nerve were something tangible that someone in the darkness was trying to tear from his grip. The softness of the earth had given him an idea. He stepped back from the quicksand a dozen feet or so and, like some huge prehistoric beaver, he began to dig.

Rainsford had dug himself in in France

when a second's delay meant death. That had been a placid pastime compared to his digging now. The pit grew deeper; when it was above his shoulders, he climbed out and from some hard saplings cut stakes and sharpened them to a fine point. These stakes he planted in the bottom of the pit with the points sticking up. With flying fingers he wove a rough carpet of weeds and branches and with it he covered the mouth of the pit. Then, wet with sweat and aching with tiredness, he crouched behind the stump of a lightning-charred tree.

He knew his pursuer was coming; he heard the padding sound of feet on the soft earth, and the night breeze brought him the perfume of the general's cigarette. It seemed to Rainsford that the general was coming with unusual swiftness; he was not feeling his way along, foot by foot. Rainsford, crouching there, could not see the general, nor could he see the pit. He lived a year in a minute. Then he felt an impulse to cry aloud with joy, for he heard the sharp crackle of the breaking branches as the cover of the pit gave way; he heard the sharp scream of pain as the pointed stakes found their mark. He leaped up from his place of concealment. Then he cowered back. Three feet from the pit a man was standing, with an electric torch in his hand.

"You've done well, Rainsford," the voice of the general called. "Your Burmese tiger pit has claimed one of my best dogs. Again you score. I think, Mr. Rainsford, I'll see what you can do against my whole pack. I'm going home for a rest now. Thank you for a most amusing evening."

At daybreak Rainsford, lying near the swamp, was awakened by a sound that made him know that he had new things to learn about fear. It was a distant sound, faint and wavering, but he knew it. It was the baying of a pack of hounds.

Rainsford knew he could do one of two things. He could stay where he was and wait. That was suicide. He could flee. That was postponing the inevitable. For a moment he stood there, thinking. An idea that held a wild chance came to him, and, tightening his belt, he headed away from the swamp.

The baying of the hounds drew nearer, then still nearer, nearer, ever nearer. On a ridge Rainsford climbed a tree. Down a watercourse, not a quarter of a mile away, he could see the bush moving. Straining his eyes, he saw the lean figure of General Zaroff; just ahead of him Rainsford made out another figure whose wide shoulders surged through the tall jungle weeds; it was the giant Ivan, and he seemed pulled forward by some unseen force; Rainsford knew that Ivan must be holding the pack in leash.

They would be on him any minute now. His mind worked frantically. He thought of a native trick he had learned in Uganda. He slid down the tree. He caught hold of a springy young sapling, and to it he fastened his hunting knife, with the blade pointing down the trail; with a bit of wild grapevine he tied back the sapling. Then he ran for his life. The hounds raised their voices as they hit the fresh scent. Rainsford knew now how an animal at bay feels.

He had to stop to get his breath. The baying of the hounds stopped abruptly, and Rainsford's heart stopped too. They must have reached the knife.

He shinned excitedly up a tree and looked back. His pursuers had stopped. But the hope that was in Rainsford's brain when he climbed died, for he saw in the shallow valley that General Zaroff was still on his feet. But Ivan was not. The knife, driven by the recoil of the springing tree, had not wholly failed.

Rainsford had hardly tumbled to the ground when the pack took up the cry again.

"Nerve, nerve, nerve!" he panted, as he dashed along. A blue gap showed between the trees dead ahead. Ever nearer drew the hounds. Rainsford forced himself on toward that gap. He reached it. It was the shore of the sea. Across a cove he could see the gloomy gray stone of the chateau. Twenty feet below him the sea rumbled and hissed. Rainsford hesitated. He heard the hounds. Then he leaped far out into the sea. . . .

When the general and his pack reached the place by the sea, the Cossack stopped. For some minutes he stood regarding the blue-green expanse of water. He shrugged his shoulders. Then be sat down, took a drink of brandy from a silver flask, lit a cigarette, and hummed a bit from *Madame Butterfly*.[8]

General Zaroff had an exceedingly good dinner in his great paneled dining hall that evening. With it he had a bottle of Pol Roger and half a bottle of Chambertin. Two slight annoyances kept him from perfect enjoyment. One was the thought that it would be difficult to replace Ivan; the other was that his quarry had escaped him; of course, the American hadn't played the game—so thought the general as he tasted his after-dinner liqueur. In his library he read, to soothe himself, from the works of Marcus Aurelius.[9]

At ten he went up to his bedroom. He was deliciously tired, he said to himself, as he locked himself in. There was a little moonlight, so, before turning on his light, he went to the window and looked down at the courtyard. He could see the great hounds, and he called, "Better luck another time," to them. Then he switched on the light.

A man, who had been hiding in the curtains of the bed, was standing there.

"Rainsford!" screamed the general. "How in God's name did you get here?"

"Swam," said Rainsford. "I found it quicker than walking through the jungle."

The general sucked in his breath and smiled. "I congratulate you," he said. "You have won the game."

Rainsford did not smile. "I am still a beast at bay," he said, in a low, hoarse voice. "Get ready, General Zaroff."

The general made one of his deepest bows. "I see," he said. "Splendid! One of us is to furnish a repast for the hounds. The other will sleep in this very excellent bed. On guard, Rainsford. . . ."

He had never slept in a better bed, Rainsford decided. ■

Notes

[1]A reputable English gun-making company, James Purdey & Sons (est. 1815).
[2]Curly wool of young lambs from the southwestern Russian city of Astrakhan.
[3]Reference to the Russian Revolution of 1917, in which the monarchy was overthrown.
[4]An East Indian sailor.
[5]A person who uses a knout, or leather flog, to whip people.
[6] Reference to Tsar Nicholas II, who was overthrown and killed following the Russian Revolution of 1917.
[7]An extravagant musical revue that began running in Paris in the late 18th century.
[8]A 1904 opera by Puccini.
[9]Philosopher and emperor of Rome who lived from 121–180 C.E.

AFTERWORD

Beth Johnson

A good adventure story holds your attention. A great adventure story makes your heart pound, your palms sweat, and your spine tingle. This book contains six of the best adventure stories ever written, containing more thrills and chills than an amusement park crammed with world-class roller coasters.

Roller coasters can give you a thrill, all right, but it's a thrill that lasts only as long as the ride. These are stories that can take up residence in your head for a long time. Months—even years—from now, during a moment of romantic jealousy, you'll imagine yourself in the famous final scene in "The

Lady, or the Tiger?" A friend's innocent invitation to "Make a wish!" will make you think of "The Monkey's Paw," and you may reply, "No, thanks!" Seeing a man and dog walking together on a snowy day will remind you of "To Build a Fire," and you will shudder.

The six stories in this book are often referred to as suspense or adventure classics. "Classic" is a word we hear frequently, but what does it really mean? You can think of a classic as a near-perfect example of something. For instance, many people would call the 1964 Pontiac GTO the classic muscle car. Or they might say Alfred Hitchcock's *Psycho*, made in 1960, is the classic horror film. As you might guess from these two examples, nothing earns classic status without standing the test of time. That is certainly the case with our six stories. The oldest, "The Lady, or the Tiger?" was published in 1884; and even the newest, "Leiningen Versus the Ants," is no spring chicken—it first appeared in 1938. In fact, the average age of these stories is 94 years! Yet there's never been a time that one of these stories has dropped out of sight. Ever since their publication, each of them has been well-known and widely read. (Note that for this edition, the language and style in some of the stories has been updated, but all the memorable details of each story are intact.)

But why? What is it about these stories that makes them so popular? What qualifies them as "classics"? Of course, that question can never be fully answered. Part of the delight of any classic is its magic and mystery, and these are qualities that can never be completely explained. But when we look at the adventure story as a *genre*—a French word which simply means "kind," or "category"—we can see two elements that make these six stories so successful.

First of all, an adventure story involves, above all, *action*. These stories are not primarily about characters' inner thoughts or emotions. They are stories about exciting things happening. In "Rikki-Tikki-Tavi," a brave young mongoose does battle with a pair of deadly cobras. In "Leiningen Versus the Ants," a plantation owner faces an army of ants, capable of stripping a human's flesh to the bone in a matter of minutes. A character in an adventure story may grow stronger or wiser as a result of what happens. But the focus is on outer action, not inner development.

Secondly, these stories present a fascinating variety of *conflicts*—just another word for the problem or struggle that the story is about. Every kind of story—whether it's a romance, a comedy, or a science-fiction tale—needs a conflict. But conflict leads to action, and because action is such an important part of adventure stories, their authors need to come up with really terrific conflicts. Let's look at the variety of conflicts presented in *Great Stories of Suspense and Adventure.*

Some conflicts are internal. That occurs when two parts of a character's personality are struggling against one another. You probably experience internal conflict every day. For instance, part of you might want to study for a test, while another part would rather watch TV. A wonderful example of an internal conflict is seen in "The Lady, or The Tiger?" In it we have a princess who is passionately in love with a young man. She is also extremely jealous. Her lover is in trouble, and she has the power to save his life. But if she does, she will be sending him into the arms of another woman. What will she do? Save his life, or let him die? The princess's internal conflict in "The Lady, or The Tiger?" is what creates the story's suspense.

But most adventure stories are about types of external conflict; for example, "man versus man." You see this conflict illustrated in "The Most Dangerous Game," in which two expert hunters stalk one another through a tropical forest. One is armed only with a knife and his wits, while the other has the advantage of guns, a servant, and hunting dogs. Only one will leave the "game" alive.

In "The Monkey's Paw," you read a blood-curdling example of "man versus fate." In this kind of story, characters try to change what seems destined to happen. Here, a happy family receives an enchanted monkey's paw, capable of granting three wishes. "It had a spell put on it by an old priest," says the visitor who gives it to them. "He wanted to show that fate ruled people's lives, and that those who interfered with it would be sorry they had." Ignoring the visitor's warnings, the family makes a first, light-hearted wish—and sets in motion a horrible series of events.

But of all types of conflict, the one that adventure writers seem to love best concerns "man versus nature." Three of the stories in this volume—"Rikki-Tikki-Tavi," "Leiningen Versus the Ants," and "To Build a Fire"—involve fierce contests between intelligent, skillful people (or, in one case, a mongoose!) and the awesome natural world. Rikki-Tikki-Tavi battles nature in the form of deadly cobras. Leiningen has to pit his intelligence against a ravenous army of flesh-eating insects. But the unnamed protagonist (the central character of a story) in "To Build a Fire" has to face an enemy even more terrifying than cobras or ants. His opponent is the brutal, merciless cold of a Canadian winter. Unlike Rikki or Leiningen, this man does not fully realize the power of his enemy. As the author writes, "[T]he trouble was that he had no imagination. He was quick and alert in dealing with actual things in life, but he did not see below the surface. He did not understand the meaning of things." There is a second character in "To Build a Fire," a dog. The dog is close to nature itself, and it does understand what the man fails to see. Reading "To Build a Fire,"you notice the continual contrast between the man's and the dog's understanding of what is happening.

With the compelling conflicts at work in the stories, it is no wonder that we are quickly pulled into their worlds. All six authors do an outstanding job of reminding us of the enormous power and pleasure in storytelling. Chances are that the thrills and chills in these stories will sharpen your appetite for more. If so, you're in luck, for you've only scratched the surface of the many wonderful stories that are waiting to be read.